THE ALIEN MAGICIAN

"Stand, fools," the magician said. More than a head taller than Kirk, he had bulging veined muscles under a bristly stubble of black hair, wings of shiny black leather, head large and more human-like, but the mouth too wide, grinning fangs. A medieval artist's vision of Satan.

"Are you the leader?"

"Yes."

"I command the truth: how many of you are coming?"

"That depends on what you do. There may be only the five of us. If you endanger us, there will be more."

He was silent for a moment. "We are in the process of investigating the weapons you brought."

"You mustn't allow that," Kirk said quickly. "They are very dangerous. On the wrong setting, they will explode with great force."

"An obvious ruse. We have the most skilled artisans at work . . ." On cue, a tremendous explosion thundered somewhere below them. Flakes of plaster sifted from the walls and ceiling.

The magician didn't change expression. "Guards-with-spears. Kill all except the leader."

WORLD WITHOUT END

A Star Trek® Novel

by Joe Haldeman

BANTAM BOOKS
NEW YORK • TORONTO • LONDON • SYDNEY • AUCKLAND

WORLD WITHOUT END

A Bantam Book / February 1979
Bantam reissue / June 1993

Star Trek is a Trademark of Paramount Pictures Corporation.
Registered in the United States Patent and Trademark Office.

ISBN 0-553-24174-5

Bantam Books are published by Bantam Books, a division of Bantam
Doubleday Dell Publishing Group, Inc. Its trademark, consisting of the
words "Bantam Books" and the portrayal of a rooster, is Registered in U.S.
Patent and Trademark Office and in other countries. Marca Registrada.
Bantam Books, 1540 Broadway, New York, New York 10036.

PRINTED IN THE UNITED STATES OF AMERICA

RAD   11 10 9 8 7 6 5 4 3

Any sufficiently advanced technology is indistinguishable from magic.
—Arthur C. Clarke

1

From the Captain's Log, Stardate 7502.9:

Nearing the end of our benchmark survey of Sector 3, we were treated to a rare sight this morning. At 0739, Antares occulted Deneb— the two brightest stars in our sky appearing to come together for an instant, red and blue fires merging.

Most of the crew turned out to watch. It hasn't been an exciting trip.

"Lopike thopis." Lieutenant Martin Larousse was babbling at Mr. Spock in the officers' lounge. "Yopoo poput opan 'opop' opin fropunt—"

"I see," Spock said. "That's not difficult to decipher. You are only putting the sound 'op' in front of each vowel."

"It's not difficult for *you*. But Earth children use it to mystify their playmates, communicate secrets."

"I doubt that a Vulcan child would be mystified."

"Well, we don't have a Vulcan child here to experiment on, do we? . . . Do you believe you've mastered it, from that sample?"

1

"Of course. If it's consistent throughout your inconsistent language."

"Well then," Larousse rubbed his chin and looked at the ceiling, "try 'uranium hexafluoride.' "

"Opuropanopiopum hopexopaflopuoporopide," Spock said without hesitation. "Allowing for your mispronunciation of 'fluoride.' "

He shook his head. "That's inhuman."

"Precisely." Spock didn't smile. "Vulcan children do use secret languages, but they are codes of gesture and intonation, constantly changing. Otherwise, they would not remain secret for long."

"They never mentioned that when I studied Vulcan." Larousse was the *Enterprise*'s linguist.

"That's not surprising. Vulcan—" Spock and Larousse stood up. "Good afternoon, Captain."

"Good afternoon, gentlemen." Kirk set his cup of tea on their table and pulled a chair over; the three sat down simultaneously.

"Another benchmark down," Kirk said and sighed, or snorted, almost inaudibly. "Exactly where it was supposed to be. As the last one was, and the one before . . . I wish one of them would be a meter or two off. We could use some excitement."

"You don't mean that, Captain," Spock said.

"No, of course not." He smiled without conviction. "But four weeks of this is enough. I'm sure the crew will be glad to move on to something else." If either Spock or Larousse knew differently—the crew seemed happy enough with the uneventful routine—they didn't say so.

"Ten more days, sir?" Larousse said.

"Nine, unless we run into trouble. Then we pick up new orders at Starbase Three." He nodded at Spock.

"We did finally get word. Sealed orders waiting."

"It must be something important," Larousse said.

Kirk sipped his tea. "Not necessarily. Whether orders are sealed is not always a command decision. A clerk can decide."

Uhura's calm voice filtered into the lounge: "All decks. Yellow alert." Kirk set the cup down with a plastic clatter, spilling some. "This is not a drill. All crew to duty stations."

Spock headed for the turbolift, Larousse blotted at the tea on his pants leg, and Kirk slapped the intercom. "Bridge, this is the captain. What's going on?"

"Captain, most of our instruments are completely scrambled—white noise. There's no . . . wait."

"What is it?"

"Everything seems to be, um, functioning normally again."

"Well, maintain alert status." He thumbed the intercom. "Engine room."

"Scott here."

"Scotty, cut the engines. We'll be backtracking at warp factor one. Stand by for either a slow search pattern or fast evasive maneuvering."

"Aye, sir."

Spock was holding the turbolift for him. "You wanted excitement, Captain."

Kirk grunted and watched the doors close. Almost to himself: " 'Speak of the devil and he will appear.' "

"We have a similar saying in Vulcan."

Kirk arched an eyebrow at his friend. "Superstition, Spock?"

"Not at all, Captain. Observation."

From the Captain's Log, Stardate 7503.0:

We have made a most remarkable discovery. At 7502.931 the Enterprise crossed an extremely strong magnetic field. All of the instruments that weren't heavily shielded were scrambled.

I felt it well within the limits of my discretion to delay our current mission in order to go back and find the source of the magnetic field. It is some sort of a vehicle, the size of a large asteroid (217 kilometers in diameter). There are sentient beings inside.

I've called for a meeting of the science staff, at 1830 hours.

Twenty-five people were crowded into a briefing room designed for half that number. Spock, at the captain's request, had invited all of the science officers and those ensigns with kinds of academic training that might be useful. Scotty brought along three engineers, propulsion systems specialists.

"Ha'e we anyone who disna' know what a 'Bussard ramjet' is?" Several hands went up, Larousse and two life scientists; and one paw: Glak Sōn, a short hairy alien from Anacontor, ensign in mathematics.

"It's simple enough: a way that an interstellar ship can gather fuel for a primitive fusion engine. We made a few of them in the twenty-first century, before the space warp was discovered.

"Interstellar space is full of hydrogen—it's spread out very thin, but there's a lot of it. A Bussard ramjet uses a strong magnetic field to suck up this hydrogen, which it fuses for power.

"They are very slow, taking centuries to go from star to star. Of the Bussard ramjets that left our solar system, two were automated probes and three were 'generation ships'—where the original crew knew they would not live to reach their destination; their great-grandchildren would finish the mission.

"The Federation has tracked down two of the generation ships and boosted them on to their destinations at warp speed. One, called *Forty Families*, has been lost for 250 years.

"We hoped we had found *Forty Families*, but it turns out that this ship is far too big. Mr. Spock has the details."

"It is very large, essentially a hollowed-out asteroid some 217 kilometers in diameter. I have prepared two diagrams. Ensign Fitzsimmons?" She turned down the lights and projected the pictures onto the wall.

"The top diagram is simply a picture of the ship. Note the direction in which it travels; it is decelerating. It is moving at only one one-hundredth of the speed of light; its deceleration is at the rate of approximately one millimeter per second per second."

"So it has another ninety-five years before it stops," the hairy mathematician said.

"And forty-seven days," Spock said.

"The inhabitants live inside the sphere, of course. It rotates, to provide them with 'gravity' via centrifugal force."

"They don't even have real artificial gravity?" someone asked. Spock looked in his direction and hesitated, then decided not to bring him to task for putting those two adjectives together.

"No, they don't. That's part of a paradox, which we will discuss in a moment.

"The lower diagram is a cutaway drawing, showing the inside of the sphere. I have charted the population density as derived from biosensor data.

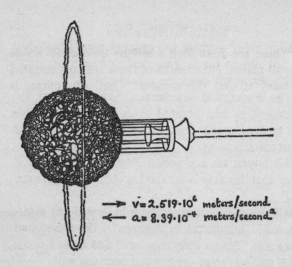

$\longrightarrow \bar{v} = 2.519 \cdot 10^{6}$ meters/second
$\longleftarrow \bar{a} = 8.39 \cdot 10^{-4}$ meters/second^{2}

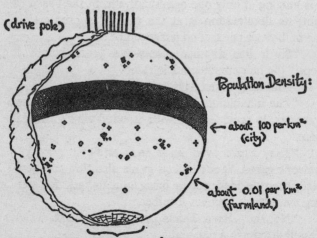

(drive pole)

Population Density:

$\longleftarrow$ about 100 per km^{2} (city)

$\longleftarrow$ about 0.01 per km^{2} (farmland)

Pole is about 10 per km^{2} with heavy concentration at the exact center. Other pole uninhabited.

"There are more than a million individuals inside that small planet. Nine tenths of them are concentrated in a band around the equator. That, of course, is where the 'gravity' is highest, though it is slightly less than one half of what we are used to."

He signaled the ensign and the lights came back up. "We have attempted to communicate with them, to no success. Everything we beam at them is reflected directly back to us." This information caused a murmur of comment.

"It is remarkable, yes. We don't yet know whether the transporter will be effective. We do not wish to beam down an inanimate object until we can follow it immediately with a contact party, so they will not have time to misinterpret our motives."

"Or get ready for us," someone said.

"That was taken into consideration, of course. They *are* a star-faring race, albeit a slow one, and it is conceivable that they might have weapons of considerable violence at their disposal.

"And there is a mystery at work. By neutrino diffraction, we found out what causes our signals to be reflected. The entire globe, under an eighty-meter layer of ordinary rock, is covered with a skin of an impossibly dense metal or alloy. Its atomic weight is apparently on the order of twelve hundred."

He waited for them to quiet down. "Supposedly impossible, yes. Nevertheless, the figure is correct. They seem to be rather more advanced in metallurgy, or physical chemistry, than they are in astronautics.

"The ship's computer has prepared a summary of what we know about this object." He nodded at Fitzsimmons and she started passing out copies of the one-page report. "Take a minute or two to read it over." He sat down next to Captain Kirk.

"Serious business," Kirk said, staring at the sheet of paper, which he had already read.

"It is indeed." Spock couldn't have failed to notice that although Kirk's expression was serious, his eyes betrayed him: he was looking forward to some action.

"Very serious," Kirk repeated, staring, smiling.

2

SUMMARY

1. At time of measurement (SD 7502.9576) the object is described by the following parameters:

POSITION:	119.70239^D, 689.4038 psc.; −1.038572^D, −0.9965 psc. w.r.t. Rigel.
HEADING:	37.903^D, 0.0127^D.
VELOCITY:	0.008401303 c (2,518,651.8 m/sec.)
ACCELERATION:	−0.000839 m/sec^2 (0.0000855 g)
RADIUS:	108,576.3 m.
MASS:	35.527835 teratonnes
RATE OF ROTATION:	0.006578 rad/sec. (once each 15^m 55.12^s)

2. Extrapolating to the past, it appears that the object has been in flight for nearly 3,000 years. Its point of origin is at the center of a tenuous globular shell of gas, which is all that remains of an ancient supernova.

    2a. This supernova exploded circa 750 B.C. There is no human record of the event, but it was identified by Vulcan astronomers.

    2b. The object (and perhaps others like it) left its system several centuries before the explosion.

3. If the object continues to decelerate at 0.000839 m/sec^2 (and to do so it must soon switch to another mode of propulsion), then it will eventually come to rest about one-eighth of a parsec from here.

3a. At that point they will be two parsecs from the nearest star.

3b. This cannot be the destination they originally planned for. All of their energy must eventually dissipate as waste heat without a nearby star to use as an outside energy source, and they will eventually freeze to death (though this may take centuries or even hundreds of centuries).

4. It may be that they wish to die. In this case, doctrine of self-determination would require that we not interfere.

DISCUSSION

+ The efficiency of a Bussard-type ramjet decreases as its velocity decreases, since less hydrogen is swept up per unit of time. Therefore, the object must soon adopt some other mode of deceleration.

Early human starships of the Bussard type used a "sputter drive" (also called Daedelus System) for the initial acceleration and final deceleration. In this phase the ships were sped up or braked by radiation pressure from the explosion of hydrogen fusion bombs fore and aft.

The large concavity (which appears to be a natural crater) that is antipodal to the Bussard-type generator on this object may be part of such a system.

+ Assuming the transporter will function properly, and a confrontation team is sent into the object, a special communications system must be devised.

Lieutenant Uhura believes she can use the particle generator on Deck Two to create a system using amplitude modulation of neutrinos.

+ The confrontation team will be beamed to the equator, where population density is highest.

3

Captain Kirk headed up the confrontation team, which was top-heavy with officers: Dr. McCoy, Lieutenant Larousse, and the security chief B. "Tuck" Wilson. The only ensign was Moore, also from security.

Wilson was an older man, quiet and formal. He centered a small black box on one of the transporter units. "Ready, sir."

It was a passive one-shot neutrino generator, which Spock had put together to test Uhura's communication system. If it were beamed down successfully, Kirk and the men would follow it.

"All right." Kirk nodded to Scotty. "Energize."

Warble, fade, disappear. Uhura's voice came over the intercom: "It's sending loud and clear, Captain."

"Let's go." The five men stepped up onto the raised dais and took their places.

"This is gonna be weird," McCoy said. "Anybody else want a pill?"

"That trank you were talking about?" Kirk said. "Did you take one?"

"You bet, Jim. It's not really a tranquilizer; just

affects the inner ear. Keep you from getting dizzy inside that spinning beach ball."

"No, thanks. I'd rather live with it." Nobody else took McCoy's offer. "Energize."

The disconcerting limbo of transport seemed to last a split-second longer than usual. What followed wasn't comforting.

Kirk opened his eyes and then shut them quickly, dizzy. He opened them again, and held on to Larousse, who was also holding on to him.

No horizon. A sun overhead, but no sky.

Looking "down" fifty, a hundred kilometers. Or was it "up"?

"We knew it would be disorienting," Wilson said calmly. "I was not truly prepared for the scale of it. Are you all right, Captain?"

"Yes." Kirk gulped and cautiously let go of Larousse's shoulder. He didn't fall.

"They're ignoring us," Larousse said. They had materialized in the middle of what appeared to be a market square, jammed with hundreds of aliens.

The creatures were slightly humanoid. They had the "correct" number of eyes, hands, feet, noses, and mouths. There the resemblance ended. They were covered with short dense fur, and otherwise wore no clothing except necklaces of ribbon, yet displayed no clue of gender. Each had a pair of wings, similar to those of a flying squirrel: continuous leathery membranes that grew out of their sides, from wrist to ankle.

Most of them were about a meter tall, though four or five were as tall as Kirk. They walked around the humans, eyes studying the ground. Every now and then one would give them a sidelong glance, but only for a moment.

They were in the center of the city, as planned. Buildings marched off uphill in every direction; to their left and right, pale green fields met the edges of the city and continued rising into the "sky," dissolving into purplish-gray haze.

The buildings were all between ten and thirty stories high, constructed of pale yellow brick and shiny metal. As the city stretched off into the distance, the buildings tilted in toward them, giving them the uneasy sensation of being in the middle of a city that was collapsing. Most of the farther buildings, whose roofs they could see, had roof gardens; the sides of many were decorated with intricate abstract mosaics of colored stone or ceramic fragments.

Each building had one or several open doors at every floor above the ground, the structures joined to one another by a graceful web of cables. The creatures climbed and glided from cable to cable; there seemed to be more of them in the air than on the ground.

The creatures had a graceful beauty while gliding, but their walk was a clumsy shuffle-and-sway. And by any human standards, they were ugly—not just odd looking, but ugly. Their eyes, bright yellow, twice the size of humans', bulged out and they blinked sideways. The nose was two red holes. The mouth was fixed in a grinning U, the upper lip fixed while the bottom jaw gaped open and shut, exposing rows of tiny sharp teeth. Their heads were elongated almost to a point, and bulged out behind.

Their hair was silky and short, brownish-red, but was missing from various places—elbows, knees, feet, hands, and the points of their heads—and where skin showed it was dead fish-belly white, as were lips and eyelids and the insides of their mouths.

Not pleasant to look at, but it's safe to say that none of the *Enterprise* people was put off by their appearance. Not only did they live in close quarters with Glak Sōn—who was also short, hairy, and less than beautiful—and the other alien crewmembers, but they would never have drawn a berth aboard the cruiser, had Star Fleet psychologists been able to detect any trace of xenophobia in their profiles.

"This is bizarre," Ensign Moore said.

Kirk nodded vaguely, watching the milling mob for some sign of interest. "Well, here goes."

He turned on the translator. "Uh, hello . . . greetings." No response. He increased the volume. "Greetings from the United Federation of Planets." The circle around them widened; the crowd noise got louder.

"I am Captain James T. Kirk, of the starship . . ."

A few of the aliens closest to them broke and ran —then, suddenly, as if a signal had been given, the whole square dissolved into pandemonium. Creatures running, gliding, screaming; fleeing in every direction away from the humans. In twenty seconds, Kirk and his men were standing in the middle of a deserted square.

"I can tell," McCoy drawled, "that this is the beginning of what is to be a long and fruitful relationship."

Kirk chewed his lower lip, thoughtful. "Well, I guess I can understand their panic. They probably haven't seen anything new in three thousand years." He stepped over to the nearest open stall, three tiers of low tables displaying exotic vegetables and fruits, and picked up a squarish purple thing. Sniffed it, wrinkled his nose, set it back. "But why no response until I used the translator? I didn't say anything particularly unfriendly. Nothing confusing . . . did I?"

"It's hard to say," Larousse said. "Some of the words might have been unfamiliar—'Federation of Planets' might not mean anything to them. But surely they know what a starship is. . . . It probably wasn't the words. We'll have to wait until we can get one to talk to us; back-translate to see whether our meaning is clear."

"Come to think of it," McCoy said, "their behavior might not be so odd. You can stand over an ant-hill all day, and the ants will work around you, more or less ignore you. Poke the hill with a stick and they all go wild, all at once."

"You think they might be members of a group mind, then? A hive consciousness?"

Bones shrugged. "It wouldn't be the first."*

"What should we do, sir?" Lieutenant Wilson said, his eyes scanning the buildings that surrounded them. "We're pretty exposed." A few dozen of the creatures sat suspended in the webs overlooking them, watching. The others had evidently disappeared into or behind buildings.

"Are your phasers set on 'stun'?"

"Yes, sir."

"All right. We'll just wait." Kirk was himself searching anxiously from window to window. Looking for what? White flag? Gun barrel? "I'd rather beam back up than use force, of course, if it comes to that."

"Of course."

---

*The Tholians, for instance; described in "The Tholian Web" in *Star Trek 5* (Bantam Books, New York, 1972), adapted by James Blish from the original *Star Trek* script by Judy Burns and Chet Richards.

The silence was oppressive, frightening. "Larousse, they were certainly talking to each other. What use would a group mind have of language?"

Larousse answered quickly, aware of the need to fill the silence. "Depends on the degree of integration. Your own brain and nervous system comprise a group mind, in a sense, if you consider all the cells as individuals. Certainly they have no need of a language. At the other extreme, human civilization is a kind of slow-acting group mind, integrated mainly through language."

"Semantics," McCoy said. "What about *real* group minds, like termites—they can't use language, can they?"

"That's a common fallacy. Termites don't operate under a group consciousness. They appear to cooperate, but that's only because of a simple set of instinctive responses."

"Might be the same thing, on a small scale."

"No." They were arguing without looking at each other. "There's no overriding guidance, no integration. They push balls of dirt around at random. When two come together, they put a third on top; instinctive response. Then another pile next to it, and so forth. Eventually they'll build a cathedral. To instinct. What was that?"

"Steps," Wilson whispered. He put his hand on the phaser at his belt. "Marching in step."

Kirk flipped open his communicator. "Kirk to *Enterprise,* Scotty, we may have a bit of trouble here. Be prepared to beam us up instantly—when Lieutenant Wilson says 'go.' "

"Aye, sir."

Wilson took the hint; he let go of the phaser and held his communicator ready.

A group of about twenty aliens marched around a corner and into the square. "One thing there's no mistaking," McCoy said, "no matter what planet, what culture . . . police."

All but one of them were armed—some with quarterstaffs, some with coils of rope. The unarmed one, who led the procession, wore three blue ribbons around his neck. The others all wore red-orange-green ones. The leader said something and they stopped marching, spread quickly into a wide semicircle, and began to advance on the men.

"Wait!" Kirk said, and a greatly amplified alien syllable echoed around the square. The police paused, glanced at their leader, and kept coming.

When they were about ten meters away, Kirk said, "Better pull us out."

"Go!" Wilson said.

Nothing happened.

"Scotty!" Kirk said. "Beam us up!"

"Disna' work—energize!" They could hear the warbling of the transporter in the background. "Again! Captain—"

Suddenly the creatures were on them, gliding in low, swinging staffs at their legs, throwing loops of rope. Moore had just enough time to draw his phaser, but it was knocked away before he could fire. Wilson wrenched a staff away from one of them and managed to stay on his feet for a few seconds, returning blows, but like all the others he was clumsy in the low gravity, and he soon joined them on the ground, hopelessly tangled up.

The police fell back in a ragged line—two of them holding their heads as a result of Wilson's handiwork —and the one with three blue ribbons stepped forward and began talking.

It was a mellifluous, lisping language, rising and falling in a pleasant sing-song. Of course it made no more sense than the chirping of a wild bird.

Kirk, whose arms were bound, made pointing motions with his head, toward the translator. It had been knocked out of his hand, and had bounced for several meters along the hard ground. "Hope that thing still works," he said.

McCoy moaned. "It might. It's made of stronger stuff than we are."

Finally the alien appeared to understand. He retrieved the translator, studied it for a moment, and spoke into it. "You need this machine to talk and hear?"

"Yes," Kirk said. "You can understand me now, can't you?"

"Of course. You are speaking the language of magicians, as I have been. It's obvious that you *are* magicians, though I must admit I didn't know that no-caste ones existed. Is that why you don't have wings?"

Kirk hesitated, then plunged ahead. "I don't know what you mean by 'magicians.' I am Captain James T. Kirk of the starship *Enterprise,* and these other—"

"What is this word 'croblentz'?"

" 'Croblentz'?"

"Oh, my God," Larousse said.

"The croblentz enterprise. What is this?"

"They don't have a word for it," Larousse said. "They don't know they're inside a starship."

"Oh, boy."

"If this is a riddle," the alien said, "I don't understand the gain of it."

"Listen," Larousse said, "we came from outside your world. Do you understand?"

After a long pause: "I think I understand. Either you are crazy or you want me to think you are."

"No," Kirk said. "Try to understand. We really are . . . we don't look at all like you, do we?"

"So?"

"We appeared out of nowhere," McCoy said. "Doesn't that strike you as peculiar?"

The alien made an oddly human gesture, spreading his wings slightly in a shrug. "Magicians are always doing things like that."

"I think we'd better arrange to meet a magician," McCoy said to Kirk.

"I'm sure you will, of course," the alien said. "You couldn't be condemned by a ven-Chatalia judge."

"Condemned!" Wilson struggled to a sitting position. "What did we do, to make you attack us like that? All we want is to talk with you."

"Maybe you really are crazy."

"Let me put it as simply as possible," Kirk said. "We live inside a world that is like yours, but smaller. We saw that you were in trouble and came to help."

"More riddles. Theology. Where is this world of yours? Under the ground?"

"In a sense."

"If you dug through in the right place," Larousse said, "you could see it, riding alongside."

He looked at Larousse for a long time, then turned away. "Guards—help these creatures to their feet."

"You *could!*" Larousse insisted.

"I think you said the wrong thing," McCoy said.

"I'm neither a fool nor a blasphemer," the alien said, loudly. "Don't try to trick me." The guards pulled the humans roughly to their feet—they were surprisingly strong—and retied their bonds, so they were hobbled but could walk.

Calming, Larousse said, "I really don't understand. Pretend I'm a newborn babe. Explain why I can't dig through to the outside."

"All right, in case this is some strange magician's test. If you dig down far enough you hit Bottom. There is no 'outside'; Bottom is everywhere. Maybe not at Below. I think you'll find out."

Kirk's communicator was beeping, but he didn't try to talk the alien into untying him. " 'Bottom' must be the metal skin Spock was—"

"Skin?" the alien said. "Metal? What metal is it that nothing can mark or dent? It's the world's end, that's all." They started walking.

"Where are you taking us?"

"To the House of Education and Justice." The translator did a pretty good job on euphemisms. "You'll be interviewed there, interrogated, and wait for the next magician, I suppose."

It looked as if the city was getting back to normal; the square filled up as they were marched out. Curious aliens watched them from above, hanging on to cables by hand or foot. There were very few pedestrians on the ground level; mostly freight traffic. There were wheeled vehicles that whined softly and left a tang of ozone behind, and pedal-powered carts like jinrikishas, and even a few draft animals that resembled small oxen. These were always led by the human-sized aliens.

"Why are some of you so much bigger than the rest?" Larousse said. Into the subsequent silence he added, "Pretend I'm a newborn infant again."

"Would you *stop* speaking gibberish! I would think it beneath a magician's station."

"You'll just have to get used to it," Kirk said. "We aren't magicians and *we did come from outside.*"

"All right, blaspheme. You won't catch me in it, though." They all huddled up against a wall while a wide creaking cart lumbered through, heaped full of pungent flowers.

"Pretending you are new . . . well, maybe you are. I've never seen a new one, let alone a new magician. You certainly haven't grown any hair to speak of." The cart was making too much noise; he stopped talking until it was by. "The tall ones are lan-Chatalia who live in the country. I am a ven-Chatalia, because I live in the city. Or maybe I live in the city because I am *ven*. You magicians live in the center lands, over Below, and are ela-Chatalia."

"You mean magicians look like us?" McCoy said.

"Oh, are you a new one, too?" They started walking again. "The masters of life can take any form, of course. Normally they look like lan-Chatalia, only a little bigger. Different faces. Better wings."

He looked at them carefully. "I would like to know why they made you without wings. There must be some purpose. It seems cruel, to my ignorance."

"I'll have to speak to Mother about that," McCoy muttered.

In less than a kilometer they came to a tall building and entered through what appeared to be an open portal, though their Chatalia used several rods on it that appeared to be keys (which he produced from a natural pocket at his waist).

They were joined by another Chatalia, who was evidently a jailer, and were herded into a lift that looked remarkably like an old-fashioned freight elevator, buttons and all. They went to the top floor.

At the end of a dark corridor was another doorless door, which the jailer unlocked. Inside, there were several low pads, too small to sleep on, a three-legged table, and an odd-looking toilet (just a depression in the floor with a drain and a dripping water hose) and an open bay window that gaped over a hundred meters of empty space and cables.

While they were being untied, Kirk asked, "What keeps us from climbing out of the window and escaping?"

The jailer—he had the same three ribbons as the guards, plus a fourth black one—said something to one of the guards, who said something to the blue-ribboned one.

"Don't make things worse for yourselves," he said. "Direct your games toward me or other nocastes."

"The extra ribbon must be rank," Wilson said. "Is that right?"

"I am losing patience. Wait—guards!" He set down the translator and said something to them. While the humans' hands were still tied, he removed the phasers and other equipment from their belts.

"Leave us a communicator," Kirk said, when the Chatalia picked up the translator again.

"Another nonsense word. Which of those is a 'repabclo'?" He pointed at the pile of equipment. "Why do you need it?"

"So we can stay in touch with the outside."

He said something to a guard, who talked to the jailer and returned the message.

"You do have some property right, even though you are mad. You may keep anything that is not a weapon." He gathered up the phasers. "From the way you used these, they must be weapons, correct?"

"Yes," Kirk said, "and they are very dangerous. You mustn't allow anyone to . . . experiment with them."

Again the shrug. "They will be held for the next magician. These other things—will you bond that they are not weapons?" There were two tricorders, medical and scientific; five communicators, and McCoy's medi-kit.

"You have my word."

"Very well. Know that if you try to escape, or harm anyone, every one of you will be killed, regardless of caste or family. This is within the law, even for magicians."

"We understand."

"You will be sent for." He followed the jailer out; the guards followed him. They locked the invisible door.

After the elevator sighed away, Kirk stepped over to the door opening and tried to thrust his hand through it. Something stopped him.

"That's strange." He pushed again. "It's something like a pressor field, but not . . ." He put all his weight behind one finger. "Ouch!" He jerked his hand back and the fingertip was bright with blood.

"Let me see that." McCoy wiped the blood off and peered at the wound in the dim light; led Kirk to the window and studied it more closely.

"Looks like crosshatching, tiny squares. Healed already." He poked his own finger at the window, and it was stopped the same way. Pushed hard, and it came back with a drop of blood. He wiped it off and peered at it. "A screen."

"Energy screen?" Wilson asked.

"No, like a window screen. But made of metal, not plastic. Impossibly thin wire."

"Acts like knife blades," Wilson mused. To Larousse: "Lieutenant, won't that sciences tricorder tell you what it's made of?"

"Should." He picked it up and brought it over to the window. "Haven't really used one since Academy —not much use to a linguist."

Kirk was still squinting at his finger. "Just activate the sensor array, channel B, and select the chemistry disc. Set the range on zero and touch it to the screen."

Larousse gave the captain a wry look and did it. "Flashes red. 'Sensor malfunction,' it says. Isn't there an override?"

"Here." Kirk twisted a knob. "Try again."

The video display flashed a confused jumble of letters and numbers—there was no compound or element recorded in its memory that matched the properties of the screen—but one line remained stable:

"ATOMIC (MOLECULAR) WEIGHT 1132.-4963."

It must be the same stuff that surrounds the ship," Larousse said. "The Bottom."

McCoy was staring out the window. "They use draft animals and have metals beyond our science. Live in a starship and think it's the whole universe. I think we'd better call Spock."

"Think he'll make sense out of it?" Wilson said.

"*Vulcan* sense, maybe. Actually, I just want a chance to confuse him."

Captain's Log, Stardate 7504.5

This is being recorded by Science Officer Spock, temporarily in command.

Captain Kirk and his confrontation team are stranded aboard the starship; the transporter only works one-way and cannot return objects from inside the vessel. Several theories have been advanced to explain this phenomenon. The most likely seems to be that the outer surface of the vessel's metal skin (which is invisible, under some eighty meters of rock) is perfectly smooth optically, to within a fraction of the wave length of an electron. How this could be done, we have no clue. But the end result is that the transporter cannot maintain a standing wave guide (the convex surface reflecting its energy divergently); thus, it can deliver anything to within the vessel, but cannot effect an exchange of information (and therefore material objects) from the inside out.

If this theory is correct, we need only breach the structure, opening a small hole anywhere on its surface, for the transporter to work. We are postponing this action, which could be construed as aggression and might possibly harm the vessel's inhabitants.

I have established a rotating shift of security personnel to stand by in the transporter room. They will beam down at the first sign of physical danger. Captain Kirk and his men are currently detained in a prison cell, awaiting interrogation.

A guard keyed open the invisible door and set down a tray with five bowls, then withdrew hastily.

Ensign Moore picked one up and cautiously

sniffed it. He made a face. "Wasn't very hungry, any-how."

"Well, we don't need it," McCoy said, crossing over with the medical tricorder. "They can beam us down field rations. I'm curious, though."

He selected the nutrition disc and put a drop of the stuff by the sensor array. "Wouldn't kill you," he said, "not unless you ate it for a week or so. Arsenic trace." They called up for lunch.

While they were eating the field rations, the guard came back and took their full bowls. He made a wing-rustling shrug and said something in a guttural voice. Moore answered "wooga-wooga," mimicking.

"Seriously," Larousse said, "it sounded like the one who was talking to us spoke a completely different language than the guards use. It was more delicate sounding, and had that peculiar whistle." He demon-strated, a half-musical hiss through the teeth.

"How could that be?" Kirk said, carefully un-zipping a package of peach slices. "Even if they started out with different languages, you'd think that in three thousand years they would've settled down to one."

"There could be some tradition at work, different languages for different activities. Church services were given in Latin for centuries, even though most of the churchgoers couldn't understand a word of it."

"Or different social classes," Wilson said. "The one with the rank-ribbon we weren't supposed to talk to."

Larousse nodded. "That happened on Earth, too. Before the first Russian Revolution, the aristocracy spoke French."

"I'd bet money that it's less complicated," McCoy said. "An alien who listened to a man and a woman speaking English might think they were speaking two different languages—high-pitched gibberish as opposed to low-pitched nonsense. It's probably just individual differences in vocal anatomy."

"I don't think so," Larousse said. "That wouldn't fool a linguist."

Wilson's communicator beeped. He flipped it open and his opposite number up in the transporter room said, "Situation report, sir." They called every twenty minutes, precisely.

"Sit-rep negative." He snapped it shut and smiled. "What language would you call that?"

"Security-ese," McCoy said. "You guys remind me of . . ."

Six guards trooped in through the doorway. They were more impressively armed than before, carrying spears and a sort of slingshot device that propelled needle-sharp arrows. They were followed by the blue-ribboned Chatalia, carrying the translator. "You will come with me now."

They followed him silently. In the elevator he looked at the translator and said to no one in particular, "I have experimented with this machine. It is very dangerous—why was it invented?"

"So that people can talk with other people . . . without knowing their languages," Kirk said.

"That is obvious. But why?"

Kirk looked at Larousse questioningly. The linguist also was puzzled. "I guess we don't really understand your question," he said.

The door opened. "There will be other questions." There was no corridor here; they stepped out into a large room.

All four walls were covered with a continuous

mosaic of polished ceramic tiles, with glittering crystals, maybe jewels, inset here and there. The bright colors clashed in jarring combinations that made no sense to the human eye. The ceiling glowed with a uniform phosphorescence.

Some thirty Chatalia stared at them from three tiers of perches. They sat with feet curled around the perch, wings drooping behind, like furry birds of prey. At the rear of the room, a single one perched above the rest.

A pattern emerged from the confusion: they were arranged by ribbons. All of them had four ribbons, three of which were red-orange-green. In the row closest to them, the fourth ribbon was black. In the tier behind those, it was red. The last tier had silver. The lone Chatalia perched above wore red, orange, green, and gold.

He spoke: "The magicians—" Translator snapped off.

"Hey!" McCoy said. "Don't we get to hear . . ."

The alien looked at him expressionlessly, and turned his back.

"Wonder if it's a court," Wilson muttered.

"I suppose we'll find out," Kirk said. "Some sort of ritual, anyhow."

The last tier was listening attentively to the obvious leader, their heads craned around at an impossible angle. All the others were looking straight ahead, except for the ones they had come in with, who stared at the floor.

When he stopped speaking, the middle (red-ribboned) tier turned around and listened to one of the silver-ribboned ones. He finished, and a red-ribboned spokesman addressed the black-ribboned ones.

"It sounds as if they're all saying the same thing," Larousse said.

"It's a religious ceremony," McCoy said. "We're all going to be sacrificed."

"Come on, Bones," Kirk said. "Try to be serious."

"Who's joking?"

In the final stage of the ritual, the middle Chatalia in the closest row addressed the group that stood on the floor. The translator turned to them and clicked on the machine.

"The chief of police would like to know whether you are ready to begin telling the truth."

"Is that all he said?" Kirk asked.

"All you need to hear."

"Then this is all he needs to hear." Kirk stepped forward to the machine and raised his voice: "We *are* telling the truth." He straightened abruptly, the points of two spears prodding his back.

The Chatalia on the tiers were staring at the floor, ceiling, walls—anywhere but at Kirk.

"Do you want to die?" the blue-ribboned one said, then clicked off the translator and spoke rapidly to the first tier. The guards released Kirk.

When he finished, one of the black-ribboned ones turned to face the next row, and the relaying process was repeated, in reverse.

"How can they ever get anything done?" McCoy said.

"They can't do this all the time," Larousse said. "It must have some ritual significance."

A minute or so later, the chief's reply filtered back.

"The chief reminds you that he is an enforcer of proper behavior, not a philosopher. Since you are magicians, he will temporarily suspend judgment, and wait for one of your own family to assess your sick behavior."

"I think it's time to start lying, Jim," McCoy whispered.

"I think you're right." He addressed the one holding the translator. "You don't seem to fear us much. Why? You know what we can do to you—or you *think* you know."

"Then you admit to being no-caste magicians."

"We admit nothing. We don't have to answer to you. But *you* will answer for much, if we're harmed."

"We've done you no harm." He moved his hands in a complicated pattern, then turned and said something to the gallery.

" 'A committee,' " Bones quoted, " 'is an organism with many heads and no brain.' This is beginning to look less and less alien."

After the procession of query and response:

"The chief will not countenance threats. He reminds you that caste takes precedence over family."

"But we don't *have* any caste."

"Exactly. So you understand, the chief may imprison you or even put you to death, unless a first-caste magician forbids it."

"He wouldn't dare kill us," Kirk said, mildly—and then remembered that his tone of voice didn't necessarily mean anything. "Don't you think there would be reprisals?"

"That's not for me to—"

"Has *any* magician ever been put to death?" Groping.

"This is outside my family's concern. Besides, you first claimed that you weren't magicians. Now you claim that family's protection."

"Wait," McCoy said. "I can make this more clear. Do you know what the word 'amnesia' means?"

"Of course."

He took a deep breath. "Now. Could we be any family other than magician? The way we look?"

"I don't think so," he admitted, "unless you are machines the magicians made for some purpose."

"I'll even admit that possibility," McCoy said slowly. "But look. As far as we know, we did come from outside—that may be blasphemy, but it *is* the truth, as we know it. We don't know anything at all about families, castes . . . isn't it possible that we are magicians with amnesia?"

After a long silence, the alien replied. "And delusions."

"So can we ask that you orient us a little, so we can at least understand what you're talking about?"

"I'll see." He passed the question up, and the answer came back. "You may, but be brief."

"Larousse, you'd better do this," McCoy said.

"All right. Explain families—how many are there, what are they?"

"There are 256 families, some of which have no members. I belong to the interpreter family. Everyone else in this room is a behavior enforcer. Except yourselves: your lack of adornment identifies you as magicians."

"How can a family have no members?"

"If its function ceases, members are not replaced when they die. Within my own memory the last of the *alfgan* herders died. The *alfgan,* of course, had stopped breeding long before."

"The ribbons identify your family?"

"Family and caste."

"And what you do for a living is determined by the family you're born into?"

Pause. "I don't understand."

"For instance, could you be a behavior enforcer, if you wanted to? Could they be interpreters?"

"Of course not. They aren't made—"

Wilson's communicator beeped. He slowly took it off his belt and looked at the captain.

"Report negative," Kirk said.

He flipped it open and the metallic voice said, "Situation report, sir."

"Sit-rep negative," he replied.

The interpreter made a hand-signal and one of the guards enforced Wilson's behavior by laying the point of a spear on his chest.

"Who are you talking about, 'negative first-caste administrator'?"

"What?"

Larousse tried not to smile. "The machine doesn't work perfectly. It doesn't know the word 'sit-rep,' so it translated the one that was closest—'satrap,' which is a kind of first-caste administrator."

"Why was he talking to the little machine?"

"It's in contact with our people outside. Part of our delusion," he added hastily. "They call us every twenty minutes, to make sure we're in no danger. If we didn't answer, they would send help."

"That's remarkable," the interpreter said, then turned around and delivered a speech. Wilson looked a little uncomfortable while they waited for an answer.

The alien gave his guard a sign and withdrew, slowly.

"The judge's opinion is that his interrogation is

becoming unsafe. Our magician comes tomorrow; we will suspend the matter until then."

"Will you continue to answer questions?" Larousse said.

"In your cell?" The alien half-turned as if to ask permission of the judge, then said, "Of course . . . if you will answer some as well."

4

Maintaining standby alert.

Thanks to adroit questioning by Captain Kirk and his team, we have a fairly complete picture of Chatalian society.

Every individual belongs to a family and has a caste level assigned to him. He may only speak to members of his own caste, or those immediately above or below him. Isolation of the individual is further intensified by the fact that each family has its own language (technically, some of these are dialects, rather than separate languages). Thus, a second-class carpenter might be allowed to speak to a second-class baker, but they wouldn't be able to understand one another.

Therefore one of the largest families is the interpreter family. Almost every transaction beyond the level of simple barter requires one of these Chatalia.

The magicians, who are relatively few in number, are exempt from the caste restriction, and may speak to anyone, although they also require interpreters. They evidently have only two castes, first and second, and first-caste individuals are rarely seen. They live in a separate area, an island which resides at the "north" (normally forward) pole of the sphere. Their main function seems to be reproduction, which the informant claims is done by magic.

The population is strictly controlled. When an individual dies, a replacement is delivered, after a time lag of about two years.

The word "child" does not translate. According to the informant, fully grown individuals are delivered by the magicians to the lan-Chatalia, who live in the rural areas surrounding the city. There they are trained, and eventually delivered to their families.

"That's about the craziest social setup I've ever heard of," Uhura said. The Bridge was idle; not much to do until Kirk and his team woke up below.

"It is unorthodox," Spock said, "but there is an admirable logic to it."

"Logic?" Sulu was incredulous. "I can't imagine a less efficient way of running things."

"In this context, efficiency was evidently subordinated to stability—which is sound reasoning, when you consider that a population of a million was to be preserved for hundreds of generations, on a space the size of a small island."

"So you think the original Chatalia were different," Uhura said. "They set up this society as a sort of a huge space ship crew—"

"And then made them forget they were on a space ship?" Sulu said.

"It seems necessarily so," Spock said. "One would conjecture that the actual working crew of the ship is the magician family, of course. The others are kept in ignorance because it would be psychologically painful for them to know they were on a trip they could never live to complete."

"Ignorance is bliss," Sulu said.

"An odd notion." The communicator chimed and Spock answered. "Spock here."

"Mr. Spock, this is Ensign Berry, in Cartography." Her voice was harsh with excitement. "We've found the wreckage of a ship on the planetoid's surface."

They had been mapping the surface in hopes of finding a portal into the planetoid. "What sort of a ship? Please give us a picture."

"It's nothing currently in use." A picture appeared on the main viewscreen, obscured by wavering streaks and sparks from the magnetic field's interference. "By its general lines, it looks Klingon."

"It does indeed. A primitive design, though. Computer."

"Working," the machine said.

"The ship pictured on the bridge viewing screen. Do you have any record of a ship similar in design—specifically, a Klingon vessel?"

"There is no such record. Captured Klingon data do not reveal designs of vessels more than 114 years old. The vessel pictured bears a superficial resemblance to a long-range cruiser of that period, which it could predate by several centuries, if our understanding of Klingon history is accurate."

"Very well. Ensign Berry, did you get any biosensor reading for the vessel?"

"Negative, sir. There's too much interference; the signal-to-noise ratio is too small from this range."

"Thank you, Ensign; that will be all for now. . . . Mr. Sulu. Make yourself a detail of three security men and an ethnologist, whoever it is who has the most knowledge of Klingon society. I believe that would be Lieutenant Sydny. And have Mr. Scott give you someone with a background in antique spacecraft—someone besides himself. Draw space suits and beam down into the vessel."

"Aye, sir!" Sulu was halfway to the turbolift.

"And Mr. Sulu."

"Sir?"

"Use utmost caution. Nothing is as it seems."

"Aye, sir." He slipped quickly through the doors.

Spock manipulated the viewer controls to get the highest magnification. "Very curious. I wonder what could have caused that sort of damage." The ship evidently hadn't been holed, but it was bent out of shape; crumpled inward, as if a large hand had closed over it.

"Tractor beams?" Uhura offered.

"Possibly . . . but it would seem that in that case the compression would be more uniform. There's something bothersome . . . of course! It shouldn't be there at all."

"What do you mean, sir?"

He thumbed the intercom control. "Mr. Sulu. Please contact the Bridge." A moment later, Sulu answered.

"Don't transport directly into the ship, not at first. There is an anomaly here. There is no reason for the wreck to remain on the surface. The planetoid is spinning and decelerating, and certainly isn't massive enough to provide sufficient gravity. The wreck should have spun away as soon as it made contact.

"So your first order of business is to find out what

keeps it on the surface. Take the security men and transport alongside. After we have a satisfactory explanation, you can go inside the craft."

"Could it be magnetism?" Uhura said.

"I wouldn't rule anything out, not yet. But I think the force would be insufficient, even if the wreck were made of iron."

"A trap, maybe."

"It seems unlikely." He turned to Chekov, who was manning the weapons station. "Mr. Chekov. If anything happens to Mr. Sulu, be prepared to react with force."

"Aye, sir."

"At my command, fire Phaser Bank One on the narrowest possible setting; pick a target anywhere on the planetoid except the drive system or magnetic field generator. We would like to have the option of repairing the damage."

To Uhura: "Lieutenant, if I am forced to initiate this action, I want the confrontation team beamed up as soon as the planetoid is breached. Will you arrange that?"

"Yes, Mr. Spock." She called up Scotty and linked the transporter room to her board.

Spock stared impassively at the image on the screen.

Sulu hadn't worn a space suit in over two years. It was a claustrophobic feeling, made even stranger by the necessity of equipping the suits with tractor gloves and boots (so the planetoid's rotation wouldn't fling them off). The four of them stepped up to the transporter dias and Sulu gave Scott a "thumbs-up" signal.

The planetoid's surface resembled the surface of the Moon, if you could sweep the Moon free of dust and loose rock. The horizon was less than a kilometer away; stars rose too rapidly over the edge. And the stars were too bright, lurid, because in the absence of any other light their suits automatically amplified starlight to make the surroundings visible.

The Klingon ship lay upside-down, to their right. They moved toward it, walking as if through thick syrup, the tractor boots holding them down.

"So far, no cables or any other support equipment," Sulu said. He had a sciences tricorder on a strap over his shoulder; because of the rotation, it stood out straight over his head.

Suddenly, the man walking next to him stumbled. He shouted "Help!" Sulu grabbed for him but missed. He drifted off into space, slowly at first, but with accelerating speed.*

"Mr. Scott—Jakobs slipped and is dropping away from us. Can you pick him up and beam him back to us?" Scotty said he would. "Everybody hold your places until Jakobs returns."

Sulu hauled the tricorder in and pointed its sensors toward the Klingon vessel. "The hull of the vessel is mostly aluminum and magnesium," he reported to Spock. "I guess that rules out magnetism." He switched to another setting. "The temperature is twelve degrees, same as the planetoid."

"Look at this, Mr. Sulu." One of the security men was kneeling, hand out. "This must be what tripped Jakobs."

---

*This is the way it appears to Sulu and the other two security men, but if you think about it you can see that the crewman was actually just flung off in a straight line, with constant velocity (the way a piece of rubber, dislodged, might fly off a spinning tire). Sulu is dropping away from *him*, since his boots keep him fastened to the planetoid's surface.

Sulu looked, but didn't see anything. He put his hand out and felt resistance. "Force field?"

Jakobs returned and explained what had happened: "I was walking toward the ship and tripped over something invisible, about here." It was the same thing; feeling their way along, they could tell that it was continuous for about a hundred meters, and followed roughly the contour of the vessel. It probably surrounded it completely.

The tricorder, though, detected no field other than the magnetic one associated with the Bussard ramjet.

Spock deduced what it was: "Check for the presence of metal." When Sulu did that, the video display gave out an alphabet-soup confusion of letters and numbers, with one line making sense: "ATOMIC (MOLECULAR) WEIGHT 1132.4963." The vessel was evidently being held inside a net of the same material that made up the doors and windows of the House of Education and Justice, inside.

They tried to melt it. The concentrated energy from four phasers produced a bubbling puddle of white-hot rock underneath the net, but the material itself was not affected.

Spock called them back, and in the transporter room the other two joined them.

Lieutenant Sydny was a young dark woman of arresting beauty: she did not like space suits. But until she put the helmet on, she could still reduce Sulu to jelly with a look.

"I don't suppose we will find any Klingons on board."

"Uh, no, no," Sulu said, staring at the floor. "The, uh, ambient temperature, you know . . ."

"The ship is too cold."

"Yes, um, exactly."

"It should be interesting, though."

"All richt," Scotty said, standing by the controls console. "She came back." Not wanting to make the same mistake twice, they had sent a passive probe into the Klingon vessel and brought it back. Evidently the net didn't have the same blocking effect on the transporter that the convex surface below did.

They put their helmets on and took their places. "Turn on your suit lights," Sulu said. They did, and Scotty bleeped them away.

Inside the Klingon vessel, the deck was covered with a centimeter-thick layer of bluish frost: frozen air. As they picked their way down a dark corridor, wisps of vapor swirled around them, the stuff being melted and evaporated by the heat from their boot soles. Twice they came to sealed doors; Sulu and Jakobs burned them open easily. The last one opened on the control room.

One Klingon had evidently survived to the very end. He was in a space suit similar in design to their own. Just before his death he had removed the helmet. His mouth and eyes were full of ice, his skin was frozen leather. The others, eleven of them, looked less pretty; they had evidently committed suicide together, and the cold preserved them in an advanced state of decomposition.

"Lieutenant Sydny," Sulu said.

She didn't respond immediately. "Yes, Mr. Sulu."

"Can you decipher the control board well enough to find the ship's log?"

"I don't know." She moved slowly past the frozen stare of the seated Klingon, and played her suit light over the control console.

"The lettering is strange, but the language seems about the same as modern Klingon. Here. They don't have a log, as such, but there is a computer entry mode that translates as 'lessons'—or 'teaching pains,' literally. I wouldn't know how to trace the wiring down, though, and separate the memory."

"I might be able to figure that out," said Ensign Masters, the antique-spacecraft expert Scott had recommended. "All right if I cut into it?"

"Go ahead," Sulu said.

It took most of an hour, working carefully with a microphaser. During that time, the three security men and Sydny checked out the rest of the vessel, taking pictures and measurements to pass on to Star Fleet Command. They found no other Klingon bodies, though the dormitory space indicated the normal crew was 113.

They beamed back up, and turned the "lessons" log over to the *Enterprise*'s computer.

PARTIAL TRANSCRIPT OF KLINGON LOG
(Note: some data erased by leakage of magnetic field through shielding. No dates were preserved, but the following excerpts are in chronological order, assuming the Klingon system recorded from the base of the crystal toward its apex.)

Suddenly our situation is quite desperate. None of the soldiers has been able to communicate from inside the planetoid, and attempts to call them back only result in overheating of the transport crystal.

In our extremity we have condescended to attempt communication with (the worms). They do not respond on any channel. We have sent fifty more soldiers down.

(Next day) Mortifying failure! I have given two fingers to the altar and still cannot find peace. My subcaptain has offered his head, good soldier. I cannot bear to record.

(Much later) Only we priests are left.

It grows colder.

In recording failure I risk blasphemy. I command all (not translatable) curses upon the putrid souls of any foreign curs who may see this, and pray (bitter) deliverance for future brothers who might learn from it.

To purify this act, I call for the heads of all surviving priests, now.

It is done. I live to watch them rot, my own most terrible penance. The facts are as follows.

We have been unable to contact the Father Ship because of the heathens' magnetic field. Over a period of (several days) we transported both companies of soldiers into the planetoid. Only then would the captain undertake the embarrassment of asking for reinforcements.

When we tried to drop back from the planetoid to call the Father Ship, we found we had been entrapped by a gauze of some apparently indestructible material. Attempting to pull free only resulted in deforming the ship, almost crushing it.

The heathens drew us in like (a fish on a line). The netting somehow drained power from the ship; when we touched the surface of the planetoid we tried to abandon the vessel, wanting to die fighting, but there was no longer enough power to transport us. Similarly, the captain attempted to explode the ship by warp overload, and nothing happened.

The captain and remaining crew, all except the priests, delivered themselves to space. We remained, to savor the terrible pain of defeat.

As (the worms) sucked the heat from our ship, we have all moved into the control room. It should stay warm here long enough for my brothers' heads to mortify, which is as it must be.

If any future brothers find this record, heed

me! This world is a bane! Do not attempt con-
quest—destroy it!

Turn our rot to ashes. Send us home to hell.

"A remarkable document," Spock said. "They
don't appear to have changed much over the centuries."

"I wonder how far they were from the planetoid,
when they got roped in," Chekov said.

Spock nodded. "A good point. We should stand
off as far as we can without breaking contact with the
confrontation team."

"I'm not sure about the transporter range under
these conditions," Uhura said, "but the neutrino communicators are definitely limited, by inverse-square
attenuation and weak-interaction noise. Maybe a thousand kilometers, probably less."

"What is the current separation, Mr. Sulu?"

"Between centers of mass, 231.59 kilometers;
from transporter to mean surface, 122.99 kilometers."

"Take us out to seven hundred, between centers
of mass."

"Aye, sir." His fingers danced over the console. He
paused, frowned, pushed the same button several times,
hard.

Resigned: "They've got us, sir."

5

Kirk and his men woke up soon after the Klingon wreck had been spotted; they listened in during the first hour or so of exploration, until the interpreter came back.

Their interpreter, whose name was W'Chaal, had grown more friendly the night before, as they exchanged questions and answers. He didn't actually *believe* their outrageous tale, but he was willing to concede that it was an honest delusion. When they started to talk about this business of a vessel wrecked "outside," though, his reply was gently firm:

"Please. For the sake of argument, I have accepted that black is white. Now you want me to believe that hot is cold. What next? Low is high? *Ven* is *ela?*"

"I suppose you're right," Kirk said, laughing. "Moore, will you persist in the delusion, and stay in contact?"

"Yes, sir."

"When do we get to meet this magician?" McCoy asked W'Chaal.

"He's downstairs now," W'Chaal said. "There are

certain formalities to be gone through, and he may have some business to conduct."

"What should we expect?" Kirk said. "Do you know this particular magician?"

"I have spoken to him. He is much like any magician." After Kirk's silence, he continued. "Reserved, cold, superior. Very conscious of his power."

"I take it his power over *us* is considerable," Wilson said. "He could have us put to death."

"Sent Below, yes. True death. Death without replacement." He paused, perhaps worried about his association with them, then added hastily, "But surely you have nothing to worry about. He must know all about you."

"I wouldn't bank on it," McCoy said.

"Last night," Larousse said, "you told us—"

"Hold it," Moore said, the communicator to his ear. "There's some trouble here."

Everyone was looking at him when the magician walked through the door.

"Stand, fools," the magician said. More than a head taller than Kirk, he was so different from W'Chaal as to be another species altogether: bulging veined muscles under a bristly stubble of black hair, wings of shiny black leather, head large and more humanlike, but the mouth too wide, grinning fangs. A medieval artist's vision of Satan.

"My God," Larousse said, standing. "He spoke to us in Klingon!"

The *Enterprise* had switched to emergency power conservation mode, normal lighting replaced by dim red safety lights. The turbolift moved slowly, and its doors had to be opened manually.

Spock slid the doors open and stepped out into the engine room. He blinked at the darkness. "Mr. Scott?"

"Over here, sir." The normal lighting of the ship was rather dim to Vulcan eyes; Spock was virtually blind now. He turned on a hand light and its beam found the Chief Engineer. Glak Sōn stood next to him.

"Any change?"

"No, sir. Whatever is draining power from us is doing it at a Warp Nine rate."

"And the rate increases, the more power we use?"

"That's right." He turned to Glak Sōn. "Tell Mr. Spock what you calculated."

"At the present rate, the life support systems will continue to function for 18 days, 4.67 hours." The short, hairy alien was handy to have around, with the computer shut off. "However, if we have to transport everyone to the inside of the planetoid, we must do so within four days, 9.18 hours."

"Even that would only be a stopgap," Spock said. "Eventually, we would have to eat their food. Dr. McCoy found that it contains arsenic."

"I *like* arsenic," Glak Sōn said.

"What we must do," Spock said, "is isolate the crew and all necessary supplies in as small an area as possible. Then shut down the life support facilities for the rest of the ship."

"Aye," Scott said. "We can set up the portable transporter in here, and close off the transporter rooms."

"Very well." He paused, then went on, almost talking to himself. "We can move down to the emergency bridge on this deck, and close everything above Deck Six. Move Medical down to the recreation area, and concentrate the crew on decks Eighteen through Twenty. Can the ship be rotated?"

"Rotated, sir?"

There was a slight note of exasperation in Spock's voice. "So that, when we come to rest on the planetoid's surface, we can take advantage of its rotation, and shut down the artificial gravity."

"Yes, Mr. Spock, I believe we can." Scotty's accent had all but vanished.

"Do so. Inform Lieutenant Uhura." Scotty went to the control console. "Can you recompute, Glak Sōn?"

"I would have to look up the exact function for the gravity generator's power drain," he said. "But this should roughly double both periods. About thirty days, or sixteen if we transport into the planetoid."

"Very well. We should have help by then." Uhura had sent a distress call as soon as they realized they were trapped. Static from the magnetic field kept them from hearing any reply.

It may also have scrambled the distress call. No one talked about that possibility.

Spock:

This is most uncomfortable. That such an emergency should occur under my command. But there was no lack of caution on my part. There were no data until we learned of the Klingon ship.

Posit: Had I initiated a separation from the planetoid immediately upon finding the wrecked vessel, might we have evaded the capture?

Inadequate data, of course. We might have been trapped soon after approaching the planetoid. Alternatively, it may be that our investi-

gation of the wreck set in motion some automatic
defense.

Subjunctive
discourse is no substitute for logic. We must accept the
problem as a given initial condition, and not concern
ourselves as to its cause until more information is
available. And then investigate the cause only as a
possible avenue to solution—not as a tool for placing
or dismissing blame! That is a purely human impulse,
and a waste of energy.

Energy: the
dilithium crystals, at least, are unaffected. Whatever
the planetoid is doing to us, the net effect is a sym-
metrical draining of the matter and antimatter in our
fuel supply. The more power we use, the faster they
drain it. Thus:

$$\frac{dE}{dt} = \frac{\delta m}{\delta t} c^2 - \frac{\delta f(W, t)}{\delta W} - R(A)t - W,$$

and the only practical course at present is to minimize
the last two terms of the equation, power output and
radiative transfer.

Sulu suggested, and many other of the human
crew must have entertained the idea, that we should
attempt to penetrate the planetoid with concentrated
phaser fire. Although I did suggest this earlier (if only
to allow the confrontation crew to be beamed back), I
believe that it would be the wrong course of action at
present. The energy drain would be equivalent to many
days of life support, and there exists the possibility
that the phaser banks would not penetrate beyond the
mysterious metal shell. It apparently is an almost per-
fect conductor of heat.

Besides, we may be at the mercy of the Chatalia for some days, even if the distress signal got through. If it didn't, it may be months before the Federation finds us (in which case we must find a way to make Chatalian food compatible with the metabolisms of the crew; otherwise only Glak Sōn will survive to be rescued.

So we must not antagonize them. Their experience with the Klingons can not have been pleasant; we bear the burden of proving ourselves pacifistic.

"I know some few words of your language," the magician continued.

Larousse had studied Klingon for one semester, twenty years before. "Not-to-be . . . language to ours. Human not Klingon. Use translator." Klingon didn't have a word for "please."

"What the hell is going on here?" McCoy said.

The magician indicated W'Chaal with a look and a flap of the wing: "He doesn't know Klingon."

"No! *Machine* translator!" To W'Chaal: "Give him the translator."

"It's blasphemy. Besides, he speaks your tongue."

"It's *not* our tongue."

"The ship," Kirk said. "Klingons must have gotten inside here."

"Silence," the magician said, which nobody understood. Larousse stepped forward and snatched the translator from W'Chaal. "Listen—"

The magician shouted "Guard!" (in behavior-enforcer language) and one stepped into the doorway. He fired his slingshot device; Larousse instinctive-

ly raised his arms to ward off the missile, and was
struck in the forearm.

"Ouch!" Larousse jerked his arm and the dart fell
to the floor—not a particularly impressive weapon.

Moore looked at Kirk, for an order. He shook his
head. "Not yet," he whispered.

"Will you listen just one second?" Larousse said
angrily. "You are speaking the language of our enemies. Our *enemies!* We are human, not Klingon."

The magician looked at him impassively, arms
folded over huge chest. He didn't say anything.

"What are you talking about?" W'Chaal said
plaintively. The magician gave him a slow glance.

Larousse took a deep breath. "From what we've
been able to find out, many generations ago a Klingon
vessel contacted you, just as—"

"*Quiet!*" The magician turned to W'Chaal. "Have
you been listening to this sort of thing?"

"Yes, master. They have many strange delusions."

He considered that for a moment. "We will talk,
later. It may be that you will have to be reborn."

"Your will, master."

"Die for hearing the truth," McCoy said. "They
ought to get along well with the Klingons."

"Guard," the magician said, "the one in the middle." The dart caught McCoy in the abdomen; he cursed
and plucked it out. "Okay, I'll keep my mouth shut."

"No, we did *not* enjoy the presence of you devils,
the last time you came. You killed thousands pre-
maturely. The memory of your attack upset all the
world, waiting for you to come again. It took many
generations to remove that memory from the *ven* and
lan."

"We are not Klingons—really!" Larousse insisted. "If you could see one, you could tell how different we are."

"I have seen many twenties of Klingons. The memory was not removed from the *ela*. You are Klingon."

Bones straightened his tunic, having examined the small puncture wound. "Don't you see, Larousse— from their point of view we do look identical. Like two different species of cuttlefish. Magician, do you have medical men, life scientists?"

"You will not direct questions to me."

"W'Chaal? Do you?"

The interpreter looked at the magician, who gave him no sign, one way or the other. "Among the magicians, there are those who practice life arts. Both *ven* and *lan* have families devoted to healing in addition to their main work, which is barbering and massage."

The doctor winced at that. "Well . . . the magician doesn't have to listen to this, but it might interest him. There are basic physiological and anatomical differences between Klingon and human. Surely someone must have examined at least one Klingon."

"Surely," the magician said.

"They have two *livers*."

"Doesn't everybody?" W'Chaal said.

"Humans only have one. Furthermore—"

"We'll count your livers soon enough," the magician said. "As for your physiology, you have just proven that you are Klingon. Otherwise that dart would have made you comatose. Two would kill you. Guard?" He appeared, aiming. "Give the middle one another." This one went for his face; McCoy stopped it with his palm, grunted, withdrew it.

"This is how you were able to take so many lives, before. Your long-range weapons worked, but ours didn't."

"Have you noticed," Kirk said, "that we turned over our weapons to you, voluntarily?"

"I said *you will not question me!*" He pointed at Bones. "You—stop that. What are you doing?"

Bones had turned the tricorders on, holding the point of the dart over its sensors. "Trying to find out what this poison is, to find out whether we will need treatment." He smiled. "Table salt, sodium chloride. No wonder it didn't affect Klingons. Or us."

"You will remain standing, while I address you." Bones stood up, slowly.

"It is you who should be grateful that you surrendered your weapons. If I thought you presented any danger to us, I would have had you killed in this cell. The information I can get from you is not worth anybody's pain or early death."

"On the contrary," Kirk said, "if you will only listen for a—"

"I may have you muzzled. Speak only to answer. Are you the leader?"

"Yes."

"I command the truth: how many of you are coming?"

"That depends on what you do. There may be only the five of us. If you endanger us, there will be more."

"You don't consider yourselves to be in danger?"

"Nothing we can't handle. Peacefully."

He was silent for a moment. "You do act differently. Before, you came simply killing. And most of the prisoners never talked."

"You see, we aren't the same. We aren't Kling-on."

"I prefer to think that it's a trick. At any rate, it will be different this time. We have your weapons from before, and we are in the process of investigating the ones you brought this time."

"You mustn't allow that," Kirk said quickly. "As we told W'Chaal, they are very dangerous. On the wrong setting, they will explode with great force."

"An obvious ruse. We have the most skilled arti-sans at work——" On cue, a tremendous explosion thundered somewhere below them. Flakes of plaster sifted from the walls and ceiling.

The magician didn't change expression. "Guards-with-spears. Kill all except the leader: that one."

Spock was doing several things at once, an occu-pation that suited him. The magician had just arrived at the cell below, and he was monitoring the conversa-tion through Moore's communicator. At the same time, he was coordinating the transfer of all command facili-ties and personnel to the emergency bridge, and moving all other personnel and necessary supplies to the lower decks around the recreation area. Deck Eight was also kept open, both because of the large emergency trans-porter on that level, and because of the flora and fauna in the small park that made up the entertainment area.

The emergency bridge was crowded. Five security men sat on the deck, around the portable transporter. Sulu, Chekov, and Uhura sat at their stations; an engi-neering ensign sat in the command chair, running sys-tems checks. Spock stood in the middle.

"Lieutenant Gary," he said to the security officer, "I think it would be better if you and your men would station yourselves at the transporter on Deck Eight. That way you wouldn't have to beam down one at a time, if trouble starts."

"Aye, sir." The men got up, stretching. "I'll detail someone to stand by to beam us down."

"At my order."

"Of course, sir." They trooped out with a subdued clatter of weaponry. The room was suddenly larger.

"Mr. Spock," the engineer said, "there's a redundancy here we could eliminate—"

The explosion was loud even through the communicator's tiny speaker. Spock stepped up on the transporter plate.

"Energize."

Spock materialized within touching distance of the magician, and touch him he did: dispassionately, scientifically, very hard, and on the jaw. The Chatalia fell back into the doorway, knocking over a guard, narrowly missing the point of his spear.

Spock drew his phaser and stunned four guards. He stepped into the corridor beyond, ducked a spear, and stunned another ten. Stepped back. "Are you all right, Captain?"

"So far, so good. We'd better get out of here."

"Agreed. This would be W'Chaal?"

"I am." The interpreter had retreated to the far wall and was doing his damnedest to press his way through it.

"We must ask you to come with us." To Kirk: "A hostage."

"We should take the magician, too. Can you handle him?"

Spock scooped him up and draped him over one shoulder. "Which way?"

They stormed down the corridor to the elevator. The door was closed, though, and there was no call button.

"Must be stairs somewhere," McCoy said. He sprinted toward an open door off to the right. Stopped short, staggered back. "My God."

People with wings don't need stairs. It was a straight drop of a hundred meters, with a skimpy-looking rope ladder dropping down the middle. The rope was about two meters from the edge, a scary distance.

They all looked cautiously down. "I must go last," Spock said. "I am by far the heaviest, with the magician. The rope might break." Five phasers materialized on the floor.

While they were arming themselves, Larousse said, "Hold it. W'Chaal, how do you call the elevator?"

He cocked his head to one side. "An elevator."

"No, not *what* do you call it. *How* do you call it?"

"Elevators don't have ears."

"Listen. If you want to ride the elevator down, how do you make it come?"

"Nobody rides the elevator down. You only ride it up."

"What if you have something heavy? You just drop it down the shaft?"

"Of course not. You leave it by the elevator, glide down, and ride back up."

"Worth a try," Wilson said. "Geronimo." He

jumped into the gaping shaft and snatched the ladder. It swung him around wildly.

Rather than going down stepwise, he bunched the ropes together in both hands, then wrapped them around his ankle, braking with the other foot, and slid down. "I'll try to get the elevator," he called back.

While they watched Wilson descend, Spock called the *Enterprise* and asked that they beam down two two-meter lengths of rope. "I apologize for the inconvenience," he told W'Chaal, "but we must immobilize your arms, to prevent your flying away."

"I understand," he said. "But I can't fly, really. Only fall gently. *He* can fly."

"Interesting." The magician was light for his size, and heavily muscled; he appeared to have at least twice the wingspan of the smaller alien. "For the time being though, I must ask you to submit."

The rope appeared and he tied up both aliens. While he was taking care of the unconscious magician, the faint sounds of some commotion drifted up the shaft.

Moore braced himself to jump. "No, wait," Kirk said. "Wilson can probably take care of it. If he . . . if they overpower him, they'll be waiting for you."

"Staying here, we are virtually invulnerable," Spock added.

"Until they haul out those Klingon weapons," Moore said.

"The weapons are centuries old. Unless they were properly maintained, I doubt that they will function."

The elevator doors opened a minute later, with a visibly shaken Lieutenant Wilson behind them.

"Hard show, sir?" Moore asked, as they got in.

"Not the fighting; I just stunned them all down. But it's a mess down there."

The bottom button took them to some subbasement; W'Chaal told them to punch the third, for the ground floor.

The phaser had evidently exploded near the elevator door. The floor was covered with purple blood. The force of the blast had blown several Chatalians to pieces. W'Chaal fainted dead away.

"This will be difficult to explain," Spock said.

Moore hoisted up the limp interpreter and swung him into a fireman's carry. "Let's get out of here!" He strode toward the door and slammed into the invisible barrier.

"Stand away," Wilson said, adjusting his phaser to the highest setting.

"That will probably have no effect," Spock said. "Not if the door is the same material as the net that is restraining the *Enterprise*."

True enough, the door was unaffected. "Aw, hell," Wilson muttered, and shifted his aim to the wall. It blasted out a hole slightly too small to drive an elephant through.

Outside, the street was deserted. A few Chatalia peeked from the upper-story windows of nearby buildings, but there was none on the climbing nets.

"Moore, keep a lookout above us," Wilson said. "Where to, Captain?"

"There." Kirk pointed to the vague outline of the magicians' island, hanging in the "sky" halfway to the zenith.

"Long way," Wilson said.

"About 169 kilometers," Spock said.

"At least we won't need a compass," Moore said. He was only half right.

Walking through the city was fairly easy, since the streets were laid out with checkerboard regularity. W'Chaal regained consciousness but remained mute when they tried to explain how the accident had occurred. He walked along with them, radiating fear. When the magician started to come to, Spock decided they ought to stun him back into dreamland—he might be more of a burden on his feet than on Spock's shoulder.

At the edge of the city they came to a broad, placid river, with no bridges in sight.

"How do you get across, W'Chaal?" McCoy asked.

He broke his silence. "You don't. It's forbidden."

"But we saw lan-Chatalia in the square. They must have come across."

"It isn't forbidden to *lan* or *ela*."

"And they fly, I suppose."

"That's right."

"That is not possible," Spock said. "The *lan* must supply food for the market, and by your own testimony they bring full-grown ven-Chatalia in, for replacement. Their wings would not be adequate."

"I didn't say they *always* fly. Sometimes they use boats."

Absorbed in the argument, they almost fell to a surprise attack. A spear struck Moore in the back, knocking him to the ground. Several other spears were in the air, but they were tumbling—evidently not balanced for throwing.

Some twenty Chatalia loped toward them; the

sweeping fire from four phasers dropped them all. Moore staggered to his feet, groaning. "What the hell hit me?"

Bones pulled up the back of his tunic; the wound was a cut about a half-centimeter deep by three long. "You're lucky. It must have been a glancing blow."

"Yeah—I sure *feel* lucky." Bones washed off the blood and closed the wound with the anabolic protoplaser.

"Are they all dead?" W'Chaal asked.

"Not unless some magician gets ahold of them," McCoy said. "These weapons can kill, but not the way we use them. This way, they only put people to sleep for a while."

W'Chaal kneeled down next to the nearest victim and stared at his face. "That's true."

"*All* of what we've told you is true," Bones said, sharply. "If you people weren't so damned . . . ignorant—"

"Cut it out, Bones," Kirk said. "W'Chaal, where do the *lan* keep their boats?"

"On the other side, of course."

Patience. "When they're here. We know there are some here. Where would their boats be?"

"I don't know. That is not my family's concern."

"You keep saying that," Larousse said. "Are you really never curious about anything? Except languages?"

"Why should I be? The magicians are curious."

"In spades," Bones muttered.

"I guess we had better start walking, sir," Wilson said. "We'll come across a boat sooner or later."

"I suppose . . . W'Chaal, the water wouldn't be shallow enough to wade across, would it?"

"He doesn't know," Moore said.

"I don't, really. There might be some place where it is shallow—but you wouldn't want to wade through. There are fish and eels that bite."

They started walking, briskly. After a half hour they spotted a boat ahead; it took another half hour of walking (always uphill) to reach it.

It was a flat raft some four meters square, propelled by poling. They cast off and started across the "river"—it was actually a lake that girdled the planetoid, and had no current—and immediately saw why they wouldn't want to wade. A black eel, longer than the raft and almost as big around as a man, followed them halfway across, grinning.

"That is very strange," Spock said. "If I were to set up an ecology for a ship like this, I certainly wouldn't include large, dangerous predators."

"I don't know," McCoy said, staring at the toothy creature. "From what we've seen, logic isn't their strong suit. Maybe it's just to keep the peasants from swimming across."

"Or it could be that they wanted to preserve as many species as possible. Like Noah's Ark, in your mythology."

"Let me take that for a while." McCoy took over a pole from Moore; Spock relieved Wilson. The security men slumped to the deck, exhausted. They were about midway, and had at least two kilometers to go.

"I'd like to have the boat motor concession here," Bones said, straining into the pole.

"Actually, sail would work," Kirk said. "There seems to be a steady breeze."

Spock agreed. "It should be a permanent condition, the water being a heat sink. Unless they choose to superimpose another weather pattern—" The magician had come to, and was saying something. Kirk picked up the translator, which was lying at W'Chaal's feet, and took it closer to the magician.

"What did you say?"

"Where are you taking us?"

"Home. To the island of the magicians."

"No. You will not get there alive."

"He's a bombastic one, isn't he," McCoy said. "We're not particularly afraid of your weapons."

W'Chaal had been silent since getting on the raft. "That's not what he means—"

"Silence!"

"Master, if they are warned—"

"Silence."

"You don't have to obey him, W'Chaal," Kirk said. "We're in charge now. Would you have us die from our ignorance?"

"That would be fair," W'Chaal said. "The ones your weapon killed died from their ignorance, or so you say."

"I told you—" the magician began.

Even through the machine's translation, a note of defiance was evident: "It doesn't make any difference, master. By light tomorrow, we will all be dead."

"What the devil are you talking about?" Bones said, unconsciously brandishing the pole.

W'Chaal flinched. "As the master says, you must not be told. We all will die, and start over."

"Maybe *you* will. I don't happen to believe in reincarnation."

"That's true. You will probably not be replaced, for your aberrations."

"Tell me," Spock said, "you actually know you'll come back? You've seen it happen?"

"Of course. Many of my friends have been replaced."

"And they come back unchanged?"

"No, they start over. They know their family responsibilities, but don't remember their former lives— you wouldn't want to remember all of eternity, would you?"

"Clones," McCoy said.

"In all likelihood . . . magician, is that so? Do you make new Chatalia from the flesh of the old ones?"

The magician ignored the question. "You are a different kind of Klingon. Your skin and ears."

"None of us is Klingon. I am half-human and half—Vulcan. Humans come from the planet Earth; Vulcans come from the planet Vulcan; Klingons come from the Klingon Empire—many different worlds."

"Babble."

"I am constitutionally unable to lie, or speak nonsense. Your view of the world is wrong, if it is the same as W'Chaal's. Or are you aware of the fact that you live inside a small world, artificially constructed, that is moving through space?"

"I was told of your blasphemy. It is the same as the ones who came before—further proof that you are Klingons."

"Where do you think we came from, if not outside?"

"The future, of course. You are magicians from the future." He looked across at W'Chaal. "You must die for hearing that, little one."

W'Chaal shrugged. "I will die tonight in any event."

"How could we possibly be magicians?" McCoy said. "We're totally different species—even our body chemistry is basically different."

"Your pretense of ignorance is annoying."

"I wonder if that eel would come back, if you fell into the water."

"Threatening will accomplish—"

"That wasn't a threat. It was wishful thinking."

6

From the Captain's Log, Stardate 7506.5

This is Lieutenant Commander Montgomery Scott, commanding in the absence of Captain Kirk and Commander Spock.

We made contact with the planetoid at 7506.1074. In accordance with Mr. Spock's orders, I had the Enterprise's artificial gravity deactivated, to save energy while taking advantage of the planetoid's rotation. The sudden change to $0.479g$ made many of the crew ill, but all recovered in a few hours.

We have beamed down two heavy-duty phasers to the confrontation team. Both of the hostage aliens claim that all of them are in mortal danger, but they will not explain why. My suggestion that we send in reinforcements from Security was turned down by the captain. He agrees with Mr. Spock that the unfortunate phaser accident may have done irreparable harm to the Chatalian image of us, and we must avoid at all costs any action that might seem aggressive.

I do not interpret "at all costs" to mean sacrificing the lives of six crew members. There

65

are twenty-two heavily armed men standing by in the emergency transporter room.

The opposite shore was a couple of meters of gravelly beach, ending abruptly in dense jungle. W'Chaal refused to get off the raft, but didn't resist when Spock lifted him off.

"There must be a path," Kirk said.

Wilson squinted, scanning the uphill sweep of the shoreline. "You'd think there'd be a loading dock, too."

"Do you know of a way through, magician?" Spock asked.

"Yes. I have flown over it."

"But you aren't in the mood to tell us," Wilson said. The magician answered with silence.

"It can't be far," Spock said, "since the raft would have taken the shortest crossing. I suggest that we split into two groups, and search in opposite directions."

"Suits," Wilson said. "Come on, you." He grabbed the magician by the arm.

The magician let out a brain-curdling scream and forced himself from Wilson's grip.

"What the hell?" In the shape of Wilson's hand, an angry purple blister welled up on the creature's shoulder.

"Salt!" McCoy said. "The salt in your perspiration."

Wilson looked at his hand, then at the magician. "I'm—I'm sorry. I should have thought of that."

"You will not touch either of us again." He looked at Spock. "Why did your touch not harm the little one?"

"Vulcans do not perspire. Our bodies have a more efficient method of heat regulation."

"I do not know this first verb."

"Perspiring is something humans, and some other animals, do to regulate their body temperature. Special glands excrete a fluid onto the skin surface; when that fluid evaporates, it draws heat from the skin."

"Disgusting." He turned to Wilson. "I command that you stop doing that at once."

Wilson laughed in spite of himself. "They have no control over it, unfortunately," Spock said. "It is an automatic reaction to an increase in body temperature."

"This is all very interesting," Kirk said, "but I think we ought to get on with the business at hand. Moore, you go with Mr. Spock and Dr. McCoy, that way. Take the magician. The rest of us will go this way. First one to find a path gets shore leave."

"Very funny," McCoy said. They split up and started searching.

After a few minutes, Spock's group found an opening into the dense bush. They waited for Kirk and the others to join them.

It was a straight path of grass, cultivated like a lawn, some three meters wide. It dwindled to a thread in the distance, as the jungle gave way to square plots of farmland.

"About thirty or forty kilometers," Kirk said, looking at his watch. "I'm sure we don't have four hours of light left . . . I wonder—"

"I must say something," the magician said. "Though I do not in any way believe that you are telling the truth, I do admit that Klingons, as we knew them, did not have this perspiration-that-burns. So you may not be Klingons."

"You finally—"

"Shut up, Bones. So you're willing to cooperate?"

"I haven't decided. The thought is strong in me that it might be best if at least one of you survived to be studied. On the other side, once you are dead you will present no threat. I am not sure."

"Add this fact to your argument, then: if we die, there will be twenty times our number here tomorrow, heavily armed and angry."

"What you say is worthless, of course. However, my indecision is valid, and to serve it I think we should live through the night."

"That's impossible," W'Chaal moaned.

"No. Not with weapons."

"But the spirits—"

"They are not spirits, exactly. You must not hear this: go down the beach."

When the little one was far enough away, the magician started. "Let me explain. As you guessed, we use life to create new life; this art has been the primary function of my family for all time.

"Sometimes mistakes are made. Custom forbids killing these mistakes. We alter their eyes so that they shun the light of day, and put them in the jungle, here."

"So the jungle is full of malformed Chatalia?" Bones said.

"I think you use an improper word. We are forbidden to judge whether a mistake has resulted in an inferior being. Our legends say that the division of Chatalia into three species was the ultimate result of such 'mistakes.'

"And it is not only Chatalia in the jungle. We control the populations of certain large animals by . . .

your word was 'cloning.' Others reproduce without help, by an exchange of genetic material."

"You make it sound so sexy," Bones said.

"I don't know that word. The eel that followed our raft is the result of both cases: the ability to reproduce naturally, which had been suppressed, reappeared as the result of a cloning accident. It happened twice, many generations ago; an accident that also made them twenty times their normal size. Now they are a dangerous nuisance."

"Natural selection," Bones said, nodding. *"Un-*natural selection."

"You expect that we will be attacked by these 'mistakes'?" Kirk said.

"We will, both Chatalia and others. The competition for food is very strong in the jungle."

"I suggest, Captain, that we spend the night right here," Spock said. "At least our backs won't have to be protected."

"No!" the magician said. "That would be certain death. The water creatures gather at the outlet of this path, hoping something will be forced close to the waterline. And they can leave the water for short periods, to attack."

"Wait a minute," Wilson said. "He knows too much about this—magician, you *fly* over the jungle. The jungle creatures never bother your kind. So how do you know so much about how they attack?"

"I have seen it many times, at dusk, from the air. Many *ela* come here when it is time to die. They must die here, if they were responsible for a mistake."

"That is a rather extreme punishment," Spock said.

Wilson shook his head. "How do you suggest we defend ourselves?"

"We must move far enough down the path so that we are safe from the swimming ones. Then we kill the small one and place his body ahead of us on the trail, to lure the mistakes. As they come, you use your weapons to—"

"Wait," Kirk said. "Absolutely not. We don't like to interfere with people's customs, but we can't allow that. It's murder."

"I don't understand."

"Don't try to understand. We can't allow it."

"But he is already dead, ever since I told him things he mustn't know. This will at least make his body useful."

"Why did you send him away, then?" McCoy said. "It shouldn't make any difference, for him to learn the truth about these 'spirits.' "

"I am not cruel. I spared him the pain of reassessment." The sun dimmed rapidly; brightened, then dimmed again. Last night, that had happened just before it got dark.

"We must hurry," the magician said, and called W'Chaal. Kirk contacted the *Enterprise* and had them send down four more phasers, and a portable lamp.

Walking swiftly forward. Kirk outlined his simple plan. "Keep the weapons on 'stun.' We'll make a circle around the hostages and set up six fields of fire. Every fifteen minutes we rotate counterclockwise, for alertness. If you feel yourself getting sleepy, say so—Bones, you have stimulants in that kit?"

"Plenty. But let's hold off on them; people get

trigger-happy." The sun had dimmed from bright yellow to bright red, turning the jungle's green to dark gray against black shadow.

"This is enough," the magician said.

They stopped and formed up, scanning the dense growth for signs of motion. The arc-lamp threw long, grotesque shadows; Kirk had another beamed down to fill in.

"Maybe the light will keep them away," Wilson said.

"I don't know," the magician said. "We have never tried keeping them away." Spock gave Kirk a significant look: the alien was volunteering information without having been queried.

There was about ten minutes of silence, while the sun dimmed out completely. They stood tense in an island of harsh glare. Bright leaves and vines trembled in the constant breeze.

"Joke'll be on them," Moore said.

"Yeah?"

"Hell, I salt everything I eat. One mouthful and they'll keel over dead."

"You don't know how happy that makes me feel," McCoy said.

"Wait," Kirk said. "That's an idea—have the *Enterprise* beam—"

All hell broke loose.

Not watching overhead, they almost lost McCoy to a twice-too-big mistake-magician, who floated silently down with fangs bared. Their magician hostage shouted a warning; three phasers stunned it and it fluttered off to one side, unconscious. While it was still in the air, three smaller Chatalia attacked, on the ground. Wilson stunned one that had two heads and four arms, with rags for wings. McCoy's was hairless, white. Kirk's target had too many eyes.

When the flying one hit the ground it toppled over one of the lamps, and settled on it. Hiss of hair burning. Moore broke formation to push it off, and was attacked by a *ven* that had a large running sore instead of a mouth. He kicked it savagely between the legs, a questionable tactic against a sexless creature, but one that slowed it down enough for Wilson to zap the thing. Unfortunately, the beam brushed Moore, paralyzing his left side. He took one step and fell over.

Wilson ran to his side, blasting the jungle at a cyclic rate, heaved the magician off the lamp, and dragged Moore back to the circle.

They kept coming. A flying jellyfish that trailed glowing barbs. A *ven* that looked normal except for a flower growing out of its chest. A rolling ball of scales and teeth. A magician with no wings. A moose with spines and fangs. Two *ela* joined by a glistening tube of flesh. One of the eel-things, humping slowly along the grass, almost dead by the time it got to them.

The bodies piled up. Action slacked off while creatures dragged fellow-creatures, stunned into immobility, off into the woods to eat them alive. Every few minutes one would attack, scrambling over the heap of bodies. Others would recover from stunning and lurch closer, to fall again.

Moore fired from the ground until the numbness wore off; requested permission to change his setting to "kill"; permission regretfully denied. Something that looked like a hairy guitar with feet managed to get within an arm's reach without falling stunned; Moore

bashed it over the head with the phaser's handle.
No one needed McCoy's stimulants.

Aboard the *Enterprise,* Scotty had deserted the
temporary bridge to sit nervously with the 22-man
force waiting by the transporters. He had made
several suggestions to Captain Kirk:

Beam down a few men to spell them.

Sprinkle a ton of salt over the area.

Send down twenty-two men—or everybody!—
and tear the whole damned jungle apart.

During lulls in the fighting, Kirk had answered
"no," "no," and "don't be crazy."

From the communicator, amplified, came sounds
of something snorting/meowing, then the phaser's
bleat and a crash.

"Situation report," said an ensign, in a voice at
once laconic and tense.

Moore replied, "Just another moose thing. Why
don't you guys stop bothering us? This is nothing but
target practice."

Scott let out a ragged sigh. "As if they c'd ken for
sure that it won't get worse, suddenly."

Lieutenant Gary grunted assent. "They should at
least let us send down something heavier than phasers.
Like the portable disrupter field—then they could get
some sleep."

"General Order One," Scotty said, half-listening.
This was the standing order that Federation explorer
parties must minimize the effect advanced technology
has on more primitive cultures.

"Somebody should read *them* General Order One.
We're flummoxed by their technology, not the other way
around."

"Aye, richt." He was staring into the space over the transporters. He loved this ship, and especially he loved the engines—and here was a vampire, sucking the life from them. With uncharacteristic force, he said, "They'll pay for this. If it's the last thing I do, I'll see they pay for this."

7

When the sun came back on, Kirk's people and the two aliens were standing exhausted in the center of a ring of unconscious monsters piled two and three meters high. Kirk slumped to the ground, and so did the others.

"Bones, you can pass around your magic pills now," he said. "We have a good long walk ahead of us, if we don't want to spend another night like this."

"No pills," he said, opening his bag. "Hold out your arm."

"Joy," Moore said.

"If you hold your arm perfectly still, it doesn't hurt a bit."

"They've been telling me that since I was five years old," Moore said. "I don't believe in the Tooth Fairy anymore, either."

(The hypo fired a premeasured dose of medicine on a blast of compressed air. It didn't hurt if you managed not to flinch at the sound, but few managed.)

Captain Kirk tried not to wince. For obvious reasons, McCoy saved Moore for last.

They clambered over the heap of bodies—which smelled like a cross between a chemical plant and a zoo —and hurried on down the path, Moore and Wilson walking backward half the time, in case some beast decided to brave the light long enough for breakfast. As they revived, though, the "mistakes" made straight for the cool darkness of the jungle, very few of them stopping for so much as a mouthful of some companion.

"Are you willing to give us some suggestion as to a form of transportation more efficient than walking?" Spock asked the magician. "Besides flying," he added, without sarcasm.

Both the magician and W'Chaal were stumbling with fatigue; obviously, McCoy couldn't help them with his shots. "When we reach the lan-Chatalia domain," the magician said, "I should be able to find us a drawn cart. But I doubt that the little one and I will be able to walk that far."

"We will carry you when necessary," Spock said, "but the longer you can travel without help, the sooner we will be out of danger."

They managed about five kilometers. W'Chaal fell first, and the magician collapsed while Moore was hoisting up the other. McCoy offered another shot, but both Moore and Spock declined.

The air was still and the morning grew hot. Moore had light gloves beamed down, to keep his sweat off W'Chaal. As they labored along, they could hear others pacing them, behind the wall of greenery. The ones who weren't carrying Chatalia held their phasers at the ready.

They didn't dare seek shade during rest stops, which Bones insisted on, five minutes out of every hour.

The interludes weren't particularly restful, since the jungle rustlings stopped when they sat down. They could feel the eyes of patient monsters, waiting for dark.

As they neared the end of the jungle, several hours later, two of the creatures did attack, staggering blindly into the light, aiming at their sound and smell. McCoy and Wilson dropped them both.

Their first exposure to *lan* country was not impressive. Blue vegetables that looked like sick cabbages struggled through hard gray soil, in no apparent pattern. Most of them were dusty and wilted, and there was no sign of an irrigation system.

"They may have some virtues," McCoy said, "but farming ability isn't one of them."

"On the contrary," Spock said, not even breathing hard under his alien burden, "it may be very wise strategy. If the crops here were edible, they would only serve to feed the jungle creatures. It's quite likely they are poison."

"Hadn't thought of that," Bones said with just a hint of scorn. But the ground and plants improved over the next two kilometers.

As they were drawing near a village, Spock woke up the magician (who verified that they did plant noxious crops near the jungle, to discourage nocturnal roving). They were walking down a straight road of hard-packed gravel, flanked on both sides by rows of some low green bush with red fruit.

W'Chaal woke up too, and the first thing he said was to the magician. "How much longer will I be allowed to live?"

"You have special knowledge now, that is not *ven* knowledge. But since you can't tell it to any other *ven* in this situation, I don't see any reason you can't live until we reach the Island." Both of their voices had a strange echo to them, because of the way they were standing. They had solved the translator problem by having another one beamed down; each alien wore one on a loop around his neck. When they were about two meters apart, though, both voices were picked up by both translators, and the result was an unnatural echo.

"Perhaps we can convince you of the wrongness of this," Kirk said, "before we reach your Island."

"Save your breath, Jim," McCoy said. "You might as well try to talk Spock out of being vegetarian."

"The two are hardly equivalent," Spock said.

Kirk rolled his eyes briefly skyward. "Magician, how do we go about finding transportation? This cart you mentioned." The village seemed to be deserted, though they could see a few *lan* working in the fields.

"We look. When we find one, we take it."

"What about the *lan* it belongs to?"

"I don't understand."

"The farmer we take it from. Don't you suppose he might need it, for his farming?"

"He'll use another . . . wait. I think I see what you mean. That he might object to our taking 'his' cart."

"That's right."

The magician and W'Chaal looked at each other and made a sound that might have been laughter. "No, the *lan* don't have any property rights, unlike *ven*. It would be more proper to say that they belong to the property, at least for the *lan* who are farmers.

"If anything, any cart we find belongs to me, since I am the closest magician. As the lives of all of you belong to me."

In a low shed next to a tall cone-shaped building, they found several draft animals and two wagons. The animals looked like huge six-legged rats, tailless. After some trial-and-error, Kirk managed to hitch a pair to the largest wagon and back it out onto the road. He loaded a few bags of feed and got everyone aboard. They freed the Chatalia's arms, tying the ropes around their ankles instead. Neither protested, nor thanked them, but they stretched mightily.

Kirk wasn't surprised to find that he was the only one with experience in handling draft animals. His own experience was the result of a curious anachronism: his father had been a politically ambitious man, belonging to the conservative Back-to-Earthers. Part of his image (town mayor with an eye on the state senate) required that he do some token farming—the more primitive, the better. But he was a very busy man, so most of the actual work was done by young Jim, after school. Trying to coax corn out of eleven acres of bad soil had given Jim an intimate relationship with the south end of a northbound mule.

"Gee-*hah!*" Twelve legs rippled into reluctant motion. A bouncy ride at first, but it smoothed out. The hot sun, always directly overhead, made him drowsy as the effect of Bones's stimulant began to wear off. He could hear the doctor snoring softly behind him.

The road stretched out straight ahead as far as he could see. He wrapped the reins around his hands twice, just in case he drowsed.

A little groggy, Kirk untangled one hand and pulled out his communicator. "Sit-rep negative. This is Captain Kirk." He looked behind him. "Security's taking a nap. Is that you, Lieutenant Gary?"

"No, sir. Ensign Dunhill here."

"Well, you can report that everything is peaceful here, with most of the team resting. We're proceeding north in a requisitioned vehicle, at about fifteen kilometers per hour. How are things up there?"

"Cold, sir. We're conserving energy . . . uh, here's the lieutenant, sir." Voice change. "Captain, Glak Sōn's latest calculations give us three days and nine hours until we have to beam everyone down. At the current rate of power drain, that is. He requested that I ask you whether you foresee any unusual use of the transporter soon.'

"No, just food. No word from Star Fleet Command?"

"No, sir. Though I'm not sure we could pick up a message on normal subspace. I will talk to Uhura and report to you next sit-rep."

"Very well." He could call Uhura himself, but that way would save energy. "Over and out."

"I'm sorry I didn't answer that, Captain," Spock said from behind him. "I was meditating."

"Well, you needed rest."

Spock hesitated. "No, Captain. It was a time for meditation. Because of the high probability that our mission will fail."

"That we'll . . . die here?"

"There are many unknown factors. But most of them offer only various degrees of failure."

"Star Fleet will find us, sooner or later."

"I don't question that. But the vessel that finds us will probably suffer a similar fate. And the one they send after that one."

Kirk rubbed his chin. "So . . . even if they did believe us—even if they made us *kings* . . ."

"Even if we could modify the food so we could live on it, we may still be trapped here for the rest of our lives. Along with whoever comes to rescue us."

"Unless they come within three days and nine hours, and can be warned," Kirk mused.

"That possibility forms one of the few optimistic scenarios."

"Tell me another; I need cheering up."

"Obviously, one is that our small journey here is successful. That we find that our magician friend—"

"My name is T'Lallis." The magician seemed wide awake.

Spock nodded. "If we find that T'Lallis is not a . . . typical magician. That others might be more willing to accept our view of the universe; might even know how to free the *Enterprise* and refuel her. T'Lallis, you are a second-caste magician, aren't you?"

The alien touched his silver ribbon. "Of course."

"The first-caste ones may be the actual pilots of the ship," Spock said. "If so, we should be able to at least describe our situation to them. Whether they will help—"

"You may never meet a first-caste one. They are mostly plant managers."

"Planet managers?" Kirk said.

"They manage the plants. Horticulture."

"That's all they do?"

"Most of them. The second caste runs the world, and takes care of rebirthing. We obey the first caste, when they ask something of us. But that isn't often."

"Interesting," Spock said.

8

DISTRESS**DISTRESS**DISTRESS**
DISTRESS**DISTRESS**DISTRESS**

This is Commander Spock of the Starship Enterprise. We are in grave distress.

On Stardate 7502.9, we discovered a remarkable artifact: a gigantic space ship in the form of a hollowed-out planetoid, moving at sublight speed through the use of a Bussard-type interstellar ramjet. It is inhabited by approximately one million sentient beings, who call themselves Chatalia.

We beamed down a standard confrontation team, but found they were unable to return. A thin shell of some metal or alloy, with a molecular weight of 1132.5, somehow prevents the transporter from working both ways.

The Chatalia imprisoned the confrontation team. They evidently have forgotten that they are aboard a space ship—it has been under way for at least three thousand years—and do not understand the team's explanations.

Complicating the situation is the fact that, several centuries ago, the planetoid was attacked by a Klingon cruiser. They remember, and believe that we are Klingons.

We found the ruins of the ship on the planetoid's surface; a transcript of its log is here appended.

Evidently the Enterprise is suffering a fate similar to the Klingon cruiser's. The planetoid is draining fuel from the ship, by some unknown mechanism. The fuel loss is directly proportional to energy use.

A warning to rescuers: the Enterprise was trapped while 123 kilometers from the planetoid's surface. The capturing device is evidently in the form of a mesh of the unnaturally heavy metal mentioned earlier.

In less than a week, the crew of the Enterprise must abandon ship, and transport into the planetoid. We should be able to survive there for several months.

We recommend that rescuers attempt to hole the planetoid with phaser fire, concentrated in a small spot. This will enable the transporter to be used, and the air loss to the Chatalia should not be significant.

We cannot live inside the planetoid indefinitely. Not only are the Chatalia hostile, but their food cannot be assimilated by humans.

This message is being transmitted on Stardate 7504.966, from 119.70238^D, 689.4039 psc.; -1.038572^D, -0.9966 psc.; at a heading of 37.903^D, 0.0127^D; all with respect to Rigel.

This is the translation of the Klingon log. . . .

Contrary to the fears of Lieutenant Uhura and Mr. Spock, the distress signal did manage to penetrate the planetoid's magnetic field well enough to be picked up by a vessel.

It might have been better if the vessel had belonged to the Federation.

The Klingon cruiser was involved in a benchmark survey, rather like the one being done by the *Enterprise*—in fact, they were following the *Enterprise* at a discreet distance. No law against it, but they nevertheless remained silent on all communication frequencies.

They did listen, and very carefully.

"Lord? Have you come to a decision?"

Captain Kulain had let the transcript fall into his lap; he was staring at the viewscreen's black night.

Without looking at his lieutenant, he said, "There can only be one course of action. Implement it."

The first lieutenant raised a fist. "Survive and succeed!" The captain raised a fist at his reflection.

After the lieutenant left, the only other person in the room was the priest Kal. "Your enthusiasm is an inspiration to us all."

"Very funny, Kal. You of all people should share my reservations."

The priest picked up his copy of the transcript and looked at the last page. " 'Turn our rot to ashes. Send us home to hell.' " He hummed the first four notes of a religious anthem. "A pious man, that one. His memory will be revered, when we bring this log home."

Kulain stood, dumping the papers on the desk, and paced, his back to the priest. "If you desire that, you had best transmit the log on subspace. We aren't—"

"Kulain. I warn you, there are limits to brotherhood. You are skirting blasphemy."

"I am a realistic man. Practical. That is why I am captain, old friend, and you are priest." He turned to him. "This stinks of death, and you know it."

"So? We all die."

"And what better way," the captain said in an unctuous tone. "Avenge the memory of a lost ship and rid the Universe of Kirk. Accidentally." The Organian Peace Treaty between the Federation and the Klingon Empire forbade armed hostilities, though either group might wage war against a third party.

"Exactly." He leafed through the transcript, averting his friend's gaze. "Our weapons are much more powerful now."

"Let me spell it out in terms that even a priest might understand. We do have more powerful weapons, true—but no more powerful than the *Enterprise* has. Do you really believe that they didn't try to fight?"

"Human psychology is very strange. It's possible they would not."

"Possible! I fought these devils, Kal, before the Treaty. They worship soft and stupid words, but underneath they are ferocious. Mark me, they tried."

"I reiterate." He folded his arms across his chest and stared at Kulain. "So we die. We die fighting."

"Good philosophy but bad tactics." Into Kal's silence, he added, "We should send for reinforcements. Allow one ship to try destroying the planetoid, with others standing back to evaluate the results. Thus the loss of a ship might be an investment, not a sacrifice. In addition, the ship might be rescued."

"And its crew denied the opportunity to die in battle."

"In the first place, there doesn't appear to be any *battle* involved. It sounds more like dying of disease. In the second place . . ." He hesitated. "A warrior who is not killed can fight again."

Kal rose. "Kulain—"

"All right. I retract that."

"You have studied humans too closely. You begin to think like one."

"Was there anything improper in the order I gave?"

"No. But the way you stated it was less than . . . forceful."

An animal sound growled up from Kulain's throat. He strode across the room and jerked a ceremonial sword from its scabbard on the wall.

"Go ahead," Kal said. "Kill your only friend on this ship. Show me that you don't need anyone."

"Kal," he said, hefting the sword for balance, "hold out your hand."

"Mr. Scott," Uhura said, trying to control the excitement in her voice, "we have an answer on the subspace."

"Put it on th' screen." Swirl of multicolored snow-flakes—interference from the magnetic field—over a vague manlike image.

"Captain Kirk?" the image said.

"Nay, sir, this is Lieutenant Commander Scott, commanding in the absence of superiors."

"My compliments, Mr. Scott. This is Captain Kulain of the warship *Korezima*. We thought it would be friendly to warn you that you are near a planetoid that we will be destroying, two days from now. We advise that you move off at least one hundred thousand kilometers, in your units."

After a moment of stunned silence, Scott said, *"We can nae move!"*

"Oh, my," Kulain said softly, "and we've already launched the nova bomb. Perhaps you should begin

whatever spiritual preparations you require for death."
The screen went blank, except for rainbow swirl.

Scott cut it off. "That pretty neatly forces our
hand. Mr. Chekov, try to find that bomb and trace
its trajectory. There's still a chance a Federation ship
may have picked up our message; they might inter-
cept it.

"Lieutenant Uhura, find Glak Sōn and begin
preparations for transferring the crew. We'll want to
take a maximum amount of food—and have Nurse
Chapel confer with a chemist about the possibility of
modifying the alien food. There might be chemicals
we can beam down with us."

"You think the planetoid's metal skin will protect
us?" Uhura asked.

"Against a nova bomb? I dinna think so. Bit I
can nae see any other course." *Nivver did I seek command.* He reached for the communicator.

They were rolling through the lazy sprawl of a
rural town. The ambience was familiar to Kirk, even
though every detail was alien: too-tall buildings of
abode, with too much space between them, the space
filled with flowers instead of grass. A thing that looked
like a cross between a cockroach and a dog rushed out
of a house and barked at them. There were no children, but every adult they passed stopped what he was
doing to stare at them. Most of them had never seen a
ven, or an *ela* that wasn't flying—let alone a creature
from Earth or Vulcan!

Wilson and Moore had their phasers at the
ready, but either no one noticed the Chatalia were in
trouble, or they weren't disposed to help.

They had gone about fifty kilometers, and the force of pseudo-gravity had noticeably lessened as they got closer to the axis of the planetoid. "I wonder how long we'll be able to use the wagon," Kirk said. "It'll be floating by the time we get to the Island."

"I suppose it depends on the behavior of the animals," Spock said. "They will find it difficult to get purchase, before long."

"Reminds me." Kirk took out his communicator. "We'll have to have tractor boots to get around."

The machine bleeped. "Mr. Scott to Captain Kirk."

"Go ahead, Scotty."

"Sair, we have rill trouble."

"Do tell . . . what now?" Scotty filled him in on the Klingon threat.

". . . accordin' to Mr. Chekov and Glak Sōn, we have aboot forty-six hours, before the nova bomb hits."

"That's within the time limit, isn't it? Imposed by the energy drain?"

"Aye. And with your permission, we'll wait until the last minute, to beam doon."

"I was going to suggest that. Help may arrive. . . . It would be far preferable for you to beam onto another ship."

Scotty was silent; Kirk knew him well enough to anticipate what he was going to say: "And don't let me hear any nonsense about 'abandoning ship'—"

"But *sair!*"

"Or abandoning us, for that matter. Your duty is quite plain." He looked at Spock with amusement. "It's going to be embarrassing enough, explaining how we managed to misplace the two top line officers, the senior surgeon, and the chief of security."

"Ensigns and linguists are easy to misplace," Larousse whispered to Moore.

"Easy to *re*place," Moore said. "That sometimes bothers me." Kirk gave him a withering look and a *shush* gesture.

Both Chatalia were listening with interest, munching on fruit they had gathered at a grove outside of town. Kirk asked for the tractor boots and dinner, then signed off.

A stack of ham sandwiches appeared, and a bowl of raw vegetables for Spock.

"I don't understand that kind of magic," T'Lallis said. "Does that come from the future?"

"It comes from the ship," McCoy said flatly. "From outside, not the future. Outside."

"What kind of magic do you understand?" Larousse asked. "What kind do you *do?*"

"Life magic, of course."

"Show me," Bones said.

"I may, once we get to the Island." He took a fold of wing-skin between his fingers and studied it. "When we do get there . . . well . . . I wish you would give up this talk about 'outside' and your *Enterprise* and such. Maybe they would let you live for a while."

Kirk cut off Bones's reply. "We've reached an impasse at that, T'Lallis. Both of us know we are telling the truth; both of us know the other is completely wrong. There's no need to talk of it anymore."

"Look at this," Bones said. He picked up the rind of a fruit W'Chaal had peeled. He had carefully torn it off all in one piece, a stiff spiral. McCoy pieced it back together, and held it with both hands, an irregular hollow globe. "Can you at least *try* to visualize it?"

"If only to help you understand our delusions," Larousse added.

"Right now, we're on the *inside* of the—"

"Trouble," Wilson said. Twenty *lan* rushed out of a building ahead, and formed two rows across the gravel road. They tilted long spears toward the approaching wagon.

"Can you say something to them?" Kirk said. "Otherwise, we'll have to shoot."

"I would," the magician said, "but they don't have an interpreter with them."

"W'Chaal, can you—"

"No." He sat up straight. "I am not a *merchant*'s interpreter!"

"If you hold the translator out toward them," Larousse said, "it will work in their language."

"Shoot them," he said. Moore and Wilson each gave a short burst, and the twenty fell like comic-opera soldiers. The draft animals froze up, refusing to detour over the flowers, so that they had to get out and stack the unconscious Chatalia on the sides of the road.

The sun blinked twice while they were doing that chore. "Do we continue in the dark, Captain?" Wilson asked from under a large alien.

"Unless there's trouble. We should be able to see the road all right, with the lights."

They could see the road, it turned out, but the road just stayed there. When it got dark, the animals folded up their dozen legs and were sound asleep in seconds.

Kirk got down and tried to coax them, with

no success. Then McCoy stepped down to help, with
the light. When the light shone in their eyes, they duti-
fully stood up.

So they moved all night, standing three-man
shifts: one driving, one guarding, and one walking
along backward with the lantern swinging in the creatures' eyes. Since Kirk and McCoy were the only ones
who could handle the animals, and Wilson and Moore
were professional guards, Larousse and Spock spent
the night either walking backward or dreaming about it
(insofar as Spock dreamed at all, or even slept).

Spock

The only reasonable approach to this problem is
to predicate success, and then work backward down the
various logical trees that lead there.

The first thing that must happen is that the
Klingon nova bomb be unsuccessful. There are three
groups of scenarios that allow this:

1. A Federation ship intercedes. The presence
of the Klingon vessel implies that *they* did receive our
message, so this may not be too unlikely. That there
would be a ship within forty hours' flight time is im-
probable, though.

2. The bomb malfunctions. Low probability; besides, they would only try again.

3. The bomb is of insufficient power to destroy
the super-metal shell surrounding us. This is the most
likely possibility, but is impossible to evaluate in ignorance of the metal's heat capacity. (There is the sec-
ondary possibility that the shell will remain intact, but
will conduct heat so efficiently as to raise the temperature to a lethal extreme.)

Proceed assuming the third set of scenarios. We are alive here, but the *Enterprise* has been destroyed on the surface.

It is possible that the Klingons will be satisfied and go away, confident that life inside has been destroyed—or at least will be desirous of reporting so. However, it is more likely that they will transport a fighting force inside. The Chatalia were evidently able to vanquish them before, unaided. With our help it should be possible to do so with less bloodshed, although it is unlikely that any Klingon will allow himself to survive.

What happens subsequent to this series of actions largely depends on the magicians.

1. They simply execute us. This is not unlikely but is a trivial solution.

2. The first-caste magicians are the pilots, and are willing to help us. In this case, our survival would depend on

A. Food supply. Strict rationing. If the local water contains arsenic, it can be removed by the Marsh process. It may be impossible to process the local food without sophisticated equipment.

B. Finding an exit to the surface. Thus we can be transported to safety when the Federation vessel arrives. Although we would be unable to communicate with the vessel, they would certainly beam down an investigating team, once bio-sensors showed life.

3. They are the pilots, but are not willing to help us. Use of force a possibility, but not advisable; we can't fight forever, and we can't take and hold the entire planet with standard issue weapons.

Our best approach in this case would be to convince them that they need our cooperation. Even if the nova bomb has no effect on the inside of the planetoid, it will certainly destroy the Bussard drive. Federation engineers would be able to repair or replace it.

4. Finally, they may not be the pilots; the ship may be either totally automated or a derelict. In this case we must try to deduce its history, and thus its mode of operation, and in this wise find a safe way to breach the super-metal skin.

All of this speculation is likely to be futile. If the ability of the super-metal to resist phaser action is due (even in part) to an extremely high thermal conductivity, then the interior of this planetoid will in forty hours attain the temperature of a supernova— for only a minute fraction of a second, but that will be sufficient.

"Spock—wake up." Larousse handed him the lamp, then hoisted himself aboard the wagon and collapsed on the floor, half asleep. Spock had been meditating, not sleeping, but he saw no reason to correct the linguist.

He stepped off the wagon and drifted slowly to the ground. They were down to about one-fourth of regular gravity now. Paradoxically, it made walking harder, not easier—especially backward.

McCoy was taking over the reins from Kirk, who stretched and yawned. "Wonder how much longer," he said.

Spock made a quick calculation. "If we continued directly to the axis at our present rate, night and day, we would arrive in seven hours and ten minutes. We do have a body of water to cross, though, which may present novel difficulties."

"We find another boat," Bones said.

"There may not be any. I don't know what happens to a body of water in a rotating frame of reference, at one-tenth gravity, but it should be interesting. And perhaps not navigable."

"In which case?"

"I have considered various possibilities. As your proverb has it, we will cross that bridge when we come to it."

McCoy shook the reins and the creatures slowly got to their feet. He looked at Spock incredulously. "Did you just make a joke?"

"Not consciously. Was it a 'good' one?"

"Awful."

Spock nodded seriously and began walking backward.

9

Soon after light, the draft animals began mewling in fright or frustration. With each step they would float up into the air for a second in the drastically low gravity, and their progress was slow and jerky. Kirk unharnessed them and shoo-ed them off in the direction from which they'd come.

Wearing tractor boots, the *Enterprise* people didn't have any trouble getting around, but the Chatalia did. W'Chaal had never been in such high altitudes, and T'Lallis was used to flying, not walking, when in low gravity. They spent a lot of time in the air, each step, until Spock took each by an arm and hustled them along.

They walked at a severe angle, as if the ground were actually a steep hill, since "up" was only perpendicular to the ground when you were near the equator.

It took several hours to get to the body of water that separated the Island from the mainland. As Spock had predicted, it presented a formidable obstacle.

The surface of the water was not well defined—lumpy, actually. It seemed to be boiling slowly, though not from heat. Volumes of water as large as swimming pools would separate from the surface, hover a moment, and slowly slide back; there was a constant mist several meters above the water, which looked dense enough to drown in. A full circle of rainbow shimmered in front of them.

"Doesn't look like a boat would do much good," Bones observed. "How do you get cargo across?"

T'Lallis shrugged. "Boats . . . *air* boats, not water boats."

"How do these boats fly?" Kirk asked.

"The *boats* fly? How could a boat fly?"

"This has a familiar ring to it," Bones said.

"How do they work, I mean," Kirk said.

"One or more *ela* tow them, with cables. They are made light by magic."

"Your 'life magic'?" Kirk said.

"Yes. It's a plant called a *hrnii*. When you put the seed in water it grows into a ball, and the ball fills itself with lightness."

"T'Lallis," Spock said, "if you open a *hrnii* ball, does the air inside burn?"

"Yes, with a hot flame you can't see. As you must know."

"A plant that generates hydrogen," Bones said. "Have you ever heard of anything like that, Spock?"

"Only on decomposition," Spock said. "Never while growing. I think we will be very interested in your magic, T'Lallis."

"If we ever get over there," Kirk said. "Even if we had one of these air boats, we couldn't do anything with it."

"I could pull all of us, this short distance," T'Lallis said.

"No . . . I would fear an accident," Kirk said with just a trace of sarcasm.

"Sir?" Moore said. "I have an idea. We could fly across ourselves."

"Have you taken leave of your senses, Ensign?" Wilson asked politely.

"No, sir. I've seen it done, on the Moon. Earth's Moon, on my last shore leave."

"I've been on the Moon a dozen times," Kirk said, "but I've never seen anyone *fly*." Wilson agreed, giving Moore a slightly dangerous look.

"Sirs, you've never been in Disneymoon, then."

"The amusement park?" Kirk and Wilson hadn't committed a frivolous act since getting their officers' stripes. "Do they fly there?"

"Now that you mention it," McCoy said, "I've read about that. It's a natural underground dome—"

"Bigger than the *Enterprise*, sir. You can fly for a long time, in the one-sixth gravity. Big lightweight wings."

"Was it hard to do?"

"Uh, I don't really know, sir. My, uh, girl was afraid to try it." Which had been a relief to Moore.

"What do you propose we use for wings?" McCoy said. "Have Scotty beam down feathers and glue?"

"It shouldn't be difficult to design wings," Spock said. "Learning to use them properly might be a different matter."

"Tourists use them on the Moon, sir."

"Park Tinney probably knows all about it," Larousse said. "She's a linguistics ensign, born and raised on the Moon."

Kirk nodded and flipped the communicator open. "See what Scotty says."

As a matter of fact, Ensign Parker Tinney had flown almost every weekend from her tenth birthday until the day she left the Moon for the Academy. She still had her wings, rolled up in her locker, just in case they had shore leave on a low-gravity planet.

The wings were lightweight metalweave cloth glued to hollow metal struts: big ones for the arms and little ones for the feet. They rolled them out on the Engineering Room floor and made careful measurements. Glak Sōn computed how the measurements had to be changed for each crew member below, and it took less than two hours to fabricate them.

"Park" Tinney volunteered to beam down with the wings and coach the men. Scott obviously didn't relish the thought of sending a wee lass like Tinney into danger while he stayed safe aboard the ship, but he couldn't argue with the necessity.

If all other things had been equal, it would have been easier to fly here than on the Moon, since everyone weighed less than half as much. But all things weren't equal. On the Moon, you could launch yourself by kicking off from a perch. On the Moon, flyers weren't encumbered by clothes; Park knew better than to suggest that these men confront their adversaries in the altogether (they did have to relinquish their boots, though, since you steer with small movements of the feet and toes).

Because of the foot-wings, you couldn't take a running start, but that turned out to be no problem. In the weak gravity it was possible to do a ten-meter standing high jump. Keep the wings close to your sides until you reach the apex of your jump, then tip forward, spread wings, flap like hell.

While the men practiced, Park had great fun doing

acrobatics. Both the Chatalia watched spellbound while she maneuvered—they had never seen true birds, since no other animal in the planet could fly, and the magicians only plowed through the air with brute force.

When everybody was able to stay aloft with little effort and make simple steering maneuvers, Kirk called them all down. Moore swooped in and braked to a feather-gentle stop; he had a natural talent for the wings. Bones broke one of his foot-wings landing, and remarked that he was lucky not to break an ankle. Park had a repair kit, though, and was able to straighten out the strut and reglue the fabric without taking the wing off his foot.

"I think our best strategy would be to stay as far from the water as possible," Kirk said. "We'll go back about a kilometer, and go for altitude. T'Lallis, can you carry W'Chaal?"

"Yes, but I don't see any reason to bring him along. He can die on this shore as well as the other."

"Bring him. We may have something to say about that."

Spock was thoughtful as they half-walked, half-glided back to their launching place. "Captain," he said slowly, "in the past you have joked with me for lacking imagination. I am afraid this is often true, and especially with the problem that confronts us now."

"Flying to the Island?"

"No, sir—the Klingon attack. There is a way that we might enhance the probability that they will fail. If it isn't too late."

"What is it?"

"Sir, the nova bomb may be a powerful weapon indeed, but like all omnidirectional weapons it suffers inverse-square attenuation: the farther away we can

cause it to detonate, the less damage it will do to the
planetoid and the *Enterprise*."

"Of *course!* We use the ship's main phasers
to . . ." His brow wrinkled.

"As you see, it is a complicated problem. We
must at any rate transport the crew, and their pro-
visions, into the planetoid. The more power we allot to
the phasers, the less power we have for the transporter
and life support systems.

"However, we do wish for the crew to stay
aboard the *Enterprise* as long as possible. Reconciling
these various aspects of the problem requires the solution of a differential equation of at least order five;
one for which I lack parameters. With access to the
ship's records, Glak Sōn should be able to solve
it."

"We'll see."

Scotty rubbed tired eyes. "Lemme see now. At
0947, we transport everybody doon, save one. At
0948, the one remaining—me—will lock the main
phaser bank on to the bomb, and blast it. Then—"

"Attempt to blast it, sir." Glak Sōn was shivering.
"There is an element of guesswork in the calculation.
We can't know for certain how powerful the Klingon
nova bomb is, nor exactly how vulnerable it is to
phaser fire. This timing represents an optimum solution, but one based on intelligence that might be out of
date."

"Intell—oh. *Spy* intelligence."

"But I still recommend, sir, respectfully, that we
not leave a man aboard. It is so unlikely that the bomb
will change trajectory abruptly—"

"That is my decision, Ensign," Scott said, a little sharply. He forced his tired brain to work. "Any calculation we can make, they can duplicate. They might foresee our logic, and arrange a course change immediately when their biosensors report that we have left the ship. This would protect them against a preprogrammed phaser attack."

Glak Sōn mumbled an apology.

"Ye've never fought them, lad—" (as good a term as any for a creature that changes gender every other year)—"so you can no' think like them." He looked at the chronometer.

"Gives us nine hours. Lieutenant Uhura, I'm going down to quarters for a while. If I'm not back by 0730, have someone come by an' give me a shake."

"Aye, sir." She smiled at him, and he thought complicated thoughts, and tried to think of something clever to say, and instead walked out blushing.

Back in his tiny temporary cubicle, Scotty poured himself a small glass of brandy, looked at it for a moment, and carefully poured it back into the bottle.

It had been a good decision to move back from the water's edge for a "running start," since there was a gradually rising thermal of warm air constantly moving from the land to the water. They rose swiftly, in a straight line at first. But the two aliens kept dropping behind, T'Lallis awkwardly holding W'Chaal in his feet, like a clumsy bird of prey. Park and Moore kept surging ahead—Moore delightfully surprised that he didn't feel the expected fear of height—and had to spill air and drop back frequently.

"Sort of fun," McCoy admitted as he drew alongside Kirk. "If they were smart, they'd sell this planet to Disney—buy a quiet little—"

"Where the hell are they?" Moore called back, beating his wings furiously to kill his forward velocity.

Both Chatalia had disappeared. In a few moments they caught sight of both: the magician a speck high above, the interpreter below, behind, falling.

Park folded wings around herself and did a slow-motion swan dive, and started swimming down through the air. In a couple of minutes she caught up with W'Chaal, whose wings were slightly extended by the rush of air, but not enough to slow him very much.

"W'Chaal! Glide! You can make it back to shore!" All he would have to do would be to turn around, facing the thermal, and flap a little.

"I know I can," he said. "The master told me to die, to fall into the water."

Glancing down, Park estimated they had about twenty seconds left. No time for argument, she grabbed a handful of fur in each hand and stuck out her elbows, which splayed the large wings out to their fullest extent, scissoring her legs for balance.

"No!" W'Chaal flailed out with both arms, striking her hard in the solar plexus. Doubling up in pain, she dropped him.

The curling-up reflex spilled all the air from her wings; she was falling as fast as he, and backward—out of control for precious seconds, until she could twist back around.

W'Chaal shouted something unintelligible and disappeared into the mist. Park splashed straight into a floating blob of water the size of a man and came out coughing and gagging.

Blinded, panic rising, half a lifetime of flying by instinct saved her. She twisted out flat, body stiff, wings full, until the coughing subsided. Feeling wet mist close around her, she ordered starved lungs not to breathe, and slowly sculled upward, toward light.

When the air on her face seemed dry and cold, she breathed cautiously through her nose, coughed twice, wiped her eyes. Pumped hard for altitude, glad that the wing fabric was nonabsorbent.

A shadow passed over her and she looked up to see Moore floating down. *"Get back, you damned fool!"* He came alongside and clumsily matched her climb rate—really not too bad, she had to admit, for a beginner.

"You looked like you were in trouble," he said.

"I'll give *you* trouble!" But she smiled.

They had gone about halfway, ten kilometers or so, when the magicians caught them, coming in from behind, lost in the glare of the sun. They enveloped the humans in a broad net of the invisible wire.

"Don't struggle!" Kirk said. "Hold your fire." Moore had taken his phaser out part-way, then reholstered it. Anyone they stunned would fall to his death.

Park had cut the backs of her hands, pushing away from the net. "What is it?"

"Microscopic wire," Larousse said, "like a razor if you press it. Try to relax."

"Looks like about thirty of them," Wilson said, shading his eyes. "I guess all we can do is wait and see what they have in mind for us."

His communicator bleeped. "Situation report, sir."

He worked it carefully off his belt, avoiding the wires. "Things are looking up," he snarled. "We're getting a free ride."

10

I have put Lt. Uhura in charge of the evacuation details, including logistical organization after transport. Following the advice of Cpt. Kirk, they will beam into the underpopulated and relatively safe farming area, where the Ian-Chatalia live.

Their first order of business, after securing the area and setting up a defensive perimeter, will be to conduct analysis of the local food and water. Ensign Amstel (Chem.) is confident that he can purify it, so that they can survive indefinitely. Otherwise, they have only 19 days' food (at normal ration of 2500 kCal/day) and five days' water (at 5 l./day).

A mass movement toward the magicians' island would not be practical, since we have only ten pairs of tractor boots remaining. These ten have been fitted to Security personnel, who have also been supplied with wings. They will serve as a rescue force, heading toward the island as soon as the perimeter is secure. What measures they take will depend on how Kirk and his team are treated.

At last communication, the team was in the hands of the magicians, having been trapped in a

105

net while crossing the body of water that isolates the island.

The evacuation will begin at 0945.0, with the transporters being energized approximately every six seconds. Transfer of personnel and supplies should be complete by 0947.5, leaving me behind to deal with the Klingons.

—Lt. Cmdr. Montgomery Scott

At 0932 Scotty was studying the list of coordinates Glak Sōn had worked out for him, alone in the control room. Uhura stepped lightly through the open door.

He looked up. "Problem?"

"No, everybody's in place. Crowded down there, though. I wanted to get away for a minute."

She broke an awkward silence, voice quavering. "I wanted to say—"

"Aw . . ." Scotty waved a hand feebly, looking at the deck.

"I wanted to say goodbye," she continued, "in case it is goodbye." She rushed on. "I've always liked you, Scotty, and I admire your courage."

"Shoo," he said, still not looking up. "An' I always . . . I ken ye to be a guid officer . . . a guid woman . . . I—"

Suddenly Scotty had his arms full of warm communications officer. For some time they didn't move or speak, Scotty standing with his eyes closed, overcome by her softness and the sweet smell of her. "Time . . . time ye shu'd be gaen doon," he said in a strange husky voice, new to his own ears.

Light chaste kiss on his burning cheek. "We'll make it," she whispered. "I don't know how I know, but we will."

Watching her leave, Scotty had time to regret a

few things he hadn't said in the past. As for the future, only the next twelve minutes were important. He sat down with the list and tried to concentrate.

Aboard the Klingon vessel, Kulain rubbed sleep from his eyes and smiled thinly at the rapidly decreasing numbers on the readout plate in front of him. "You'll have a medal for this, Karez."

The science officer nodded. "It was one of several possible courses of action. Probably the one I would have advised myself, if I were cowardly."

Or if you wanted the maximum number of soldiers fighting inside, Kulain thought. "Begin the evasive action now."

He switched on the viewscreen and stared at the image of the trapped *Enterprise*. "If they hope to save the ship," he said, "they should start firing about now."

Scotty propped the figures next to the viewscreen and turned it on. Glak Sōn's figures were based on a "random walk" evasion pattern, which the Klingons had used in the past. Both hands on the keyboard, foot on the firing switch, he stared at the image of the nova bomb. There was about one twentieth of a second time lag, so he'd have to "lead" the bomb, the way a duck hunter aims ahead of his prey.

The image twitched sideways: Scotty picked the figure for that angular displacement off the sheet, typed in three quick digits, and stamped on the firing switch.

A pale thread of light touched the bomb. There was no visible effect.

Sweat springing out on his face, he waited for the next twitch, and did it again. This time there was not even the thread.

He shouted a single word at the console and kicked it, hurting his toe. Turned off the viewscreen and limped to the portable transporter.

"Energize," he said. A red light started blinking on the automatic control. Not enough power. If he tried to beam down he would simply be disassociated into random particles, never to be reassembled.

Maybe better than nine hours' waiting for a nova bomb. Which would do the same thing.

He started to call Uhura and then decided to wait a bit. There'd be a real circus going on down there now. Besides, he had a few chores.

He walked down to the Galley and got a few rations, then closed it off. Then to his quarters, to pick up a bottle of Denebian brandy—should last nine hours. Eventually he shut off life support for everything save the emergency control room and Deck Eight, where the trees and streams were. He had to conserve power, since it was still remotely possible that a Federation ship would come to the rescue and save at least him from the Klingon attack.

More likely, he would be the first one to die, by a fraction of a nanosecond.

In the control room, he flipped a few switches to enable him to take and receive all calls through his hand communicator in the entertainment area. Then he took the lift there, found a small glass of exquisite crystal, sat on the cool grass with his back against a tree, poured a drink, and sipped at it. Set it carefully on the ground.

"This is the *Enterprise* to Uhura, Jim; whoever's listening down there.

"There must have been some error in the calculations. Although we did hit the nova bomb, there wasn't enough power left to do any damage. Neither was there enough power to beam me down afterward.

"Glak Sōn, I don't blame you for this, no' in the slightest. Ye warned me—besides, your figgers for the random walk worked foin."

He chose his words carefully. "I can't talk long. This neutrino thing pulls thirty times the energy of a reg'lar communicator. If I call again it will be because help has come. I miss you and goodbye."

"I can not understand," Glak Sōn said, trembling with some alien emotion—perhaps not alien—"I included quite a large margin for error."

Uhura reached down and patted him on the shoulder, occupied with her own thoughts. "It must have been the data."

"I do not see how. I had to be so sure." He turned and walked away. "I liked him."

Four hundred people milling around in a field of blue cabbages, giving and taking orders. If they were Bantu, Uhura thought, they would do the sensible thing: sit and wait quietly for nine hours. If they survived the nova bomb, *then* would be the time to set up food and water distribution systems, dig latrines, assign "billets"; the only urgent things to be done right now had to do with the natives—set up perimeter guards, mainly. She also detailed some people to carefully harvest and stack the cabbages in their immediate area so they wouldn't be trampled.

She sat cross-legged on the dry ground and watched her orders being carried out. She had faced death before and had that pretty well sorted out, but she didn't care for this feeling of impotence, knowing to the minute and second when the blow would come, unable to stay it.

At least there was a familiar African feeling of paradox about it. Not "paradox," quite; there wasn't any precise English word for it. It was sitting inside a tiny ball where the sky was the ground, closed in completely yet lost in the vastness between the stars. It was this placid, idiotically well-manicured cabbage field, where they had all come to share the sort of death usually reserved for stars.

It was the odd family-feeling she had, being in charge of these hundreds of brothers, sisters, children —having tacitly given up motherhood for the Federation and the *Enterprise* (to her family's disappointment) and now mothering the whole ship's brood.

It made her think of a tale she'd learned from her great-grandmother's sister:

The first man and woman lived happily in Heaven.

One day God told them they were going to earth, and asked whether they would rather have the fate of the moon, or the fate of a banana.

They were not sure.

He explained: the moon grows, then wanes, then dies. But it always comes back.

The banana, while it lives, sends out shoots, which accompany it while it waxes and wanes, and surround it when it dies. But it dies forever, except that its children still live.

So we may always be reborn, they said, but live and die alone; or we may share life with children, but die one time.

As you choose.

Which way is better? they asked.

I won't tell you. All of the animals have chosen one way. Since you are my favorites I saved you for last.

Which way did the animals choose?

God laughed. I won't tell you that, either.

The man wanted the moon's way, arguing from his head and his fears. The woman wanted the banana's way, arguing from her womb and her hopes. The man used words, and the woman did not: thus, they gave us life, and death.

Her great-grand-aunt wouldn't have been surprised to learn of the Chatalia, Uhura thought. Just people who chose the way of the moon.

11

They were only a few minutes away from the Island. "I guess we better put on the boots," Kirk said, wriggling his right arm out of the wing and reaching back to where the boots were stuffed under his belt. "Can we fly at all without the foot-wings, Ensign?"

"You can stay aloft," Park said. "You just can't steer very well."

"Can't draw and fire too well, either," Wilson said, "unless we give up the wings altogether."

"That's true," Larousse said, "but they'll probably disarm us as soon as we land, anyhow."

"Or try to," Wilson said.

"We'll have to assess the situation," Kirk said. "If we still had Scotty to bail us out with the transporter, we could surrender the weapons without too much worry. But these are the only ones we're going to get, now."

"If they were humans," McCoy said, "I'd say hand over the phasers and rely on their curiosity to keep us alive, at least for a while. But I'm not sure they really have any."

"And they sure kill their own kind easily enough," Park added.

"Wait," Wilson said. "Insurance—two of us still have two weapons each, since the phaser rifles were beamed down. I can hide the phaser in the top of my boot, and just surrender the larger weapons—Moore, you still have your phaser?"

Moore smiled innocently. "Already tucked away, sir."

"So we'll play it by ear," Kirk said. "If they obviously plan to kill us out of hand, we'll hold them off as long as the phaser crystals last." Everybody knew, but didn't mention, that the crystals would likely outlast the planetoid's inhabitants. "If they want to talk, but want us disarmed, we give up all but the two hidden weapons."

"Three, sir," Park said, blushing a little. "Mr. Scott insisted that I carry a backup." It was strapped to her forearm, under the sleeve of her tunic. "Should I give it to someone else? I've never used one, except for training."

"No," Spock said. "Since you are by far the smallest, they may think you are the least dangerous."

"But I *am!*"

They were close enough to land now to see their welcoming committee. Most of them were armed with spears. All were magicians; one had the gold ribbon of rank. One was T'Lallis—or might have been some other *ela,* with the translator around his neck. The only translator they had, now.

Free of the net, they drifted to the ground. There was virtually no centrifugal "gravity" here; they landed feet-first because of the tractor boots.

"Hell," Moore whispered, "we could take them with our bare hands." The magicians had spears, but needed their wings to move. They floated around the crew like ugly angels.

"I don't know," Wilson said. "This is their natural element." But it was hard to see how they might use their spears effectively, the points bobbing up and down as they approached.

The first-caste magician said something incomprehensible. T'Lallis swam over and held out the translator, and he repeated it.

"You are prisoners now. Any aggression will be rewarded with death." T'Lallis whispered something. "Put your hands in front of you and allow us to take your weapons."

Three unarmed magicians moved in behind them, to disarm them.

"T'Lallis," Kirk said, "tell them to leave our communicators."

"No. You can use them to summon new weapons; I saw you do it."

"Remember not to touch their skin," the first-caste one said. "What is in those bags?"

"This is medical equipment," Bones said. He pointed to the ones Larousse and Park carried, shoulder-slung. "Those are scientific measuring devices and food and water."

"Search them." The three looked through the tricorder kits and the food bag, and were evidently satisfied. They brought the phasers and rifles back to him, having missed the hidden ones.

The magician inspected one of the phasers. "This is what killed so many *ven* at the House of Education and Justice?"

"Yes," Kirk said, "because they ignored our warning about it."

He handed it back to the second-caste searcher. "How are you able to stand there, as if you were downworld, and had force at your feet?"

"Just magic," Kirk said.

"That isn't enough."

"Good! We can bargain. The more you tell us, the more we'll tell you."

The magician was silent for a minute. "We can try, perhaps. Tell me more about standing."

"We wear 'tractor boots'—"

"Nonsense word."

"I know. Since you don't have a word for it, the translator can't do anything but make up a word. I'll show you, though." He unzipped the boots and stepped out, drifting a couple of meters. Then he clumsily flew himself down and put the boots back on.

"I see how you do it," the magician said, "the things on your feet are sticky. I don't understand why, though. You can fly; why deny yourselves the freedom?"

"We aren't used to flying. Where we live there is always force at your feet."

"As with the *ven* and *lan*."

"Something like that; a different kind of force, though. My question: What do the first-caste *ela* know that the second-caste don't?"

"I can't answer that with all of these people around. I'm not sure I could tell you anyway."

"Send them away, and try."

"No. I think that would be dangerous. Ask a different question."

"May I, Captain?" Spock said. Kirk nodded. "A

small question. Are you aware that we are not Klingons?"

"We think you are a different kind of Klingon," he answered without hesitation. "The ones who came before acted differently. Which doesn't mean we can trust you."

"All right," Kirk said. "That seems a fair exchange. Ask another."

"This weapon." He took it from the second-caste beside him. "How is it that sometimes it kills and sometimes it only puts to sleep?"

"There's a dial," Kirk began.

"Nonsense word."

"Let me try," Larousse said. "There's a way you can tell it what to do. Normally, we don't want it to kill anybody. But it can kill by burning, or even explode itself, if you tell it the wrong thing."

"We have made animals like that." He weighed the weapon in his hand. "This doesn't live, though."

"No. It's a machine."

"I don't understand." He drifted over and handed it to Larousse. "Kill someone. Not me."

"What?"

"One of the second-caste."

Larousse looked at the phaser, then at the magician. "I . . . we . . . don't kill without reason."

"This is a reason."

"Not—not good enough."

"They're just security." Wilson and Moore exchanged looks. "They won't be gone long."

"Spopock," he said in Op. "Whopat shopould opI dopoo?" *Spock—what should I do?*

"What was that?" The translator was set up for English, of course.

"Gopive opit bopack." *Give it back.*

The magician sculled backward. "Try this: Guard, kill the little one."

One of the guards gave a flip of his wings and flew straight toward Park, spear stiff in front of him.

"Take 'em!" Wilson shouted. He and Moore fumbled for their hidden phasers, hampered by the wings. Park's was more accessible: she had it out just as the point of the spear drove into her abdomen.

She fired, and the guard exploded into a bloody purple blossom, only the head and limbs intact.

She gave a single grunt of pain, maybe confusion; the force of the blow was enough to break the hold of the tractors, and she sailed slowly away, tumbling, trailing a viscous ribbon of blood.

Moore and Wilson were back-to-back, down on one knee, firing. They stunned the armed ones first, and then the other guards. Then Moore stood up and faced the magician. He spun the force-setting wheel up to "9."

"Murderer." He took aim.

"Don't do it, Moore," Kirk snapped. "Maybe later."

McCoy dashed over to Tinney and gentled her to the ground. He opened his medical kit and used scissors to snip away cloth, leaving the spear head in the wound.

She was in grave shock—skin grayish, only the whites of her eyes showing, breathing in shallow rapid gasps. McCoy set his tricorder on "tomography" and looked at the wound from several angles.

"Bad," he said. "Retroperitoneal, opened the inferior vena cava. You guys have paramedic training?"

"Yes," Moore and Wilson said simultaneously.

"Have to move fast. Get on both sides here." He slipped the sterile field grid under the small of her back. "Listen once." He gave her an anaesthetic shot. "I have to make a rather long incision here. Vena cava's about eight centimeters in. You have to hold the lips of the wound apart while I dig; just pull gently on the skin, like this. Won't be pretty." It was already rather gruesome, red foam bubbling everywhere but "down," but became rapidly worse when McCoy jerked out the spear and went to work.

It took about sixty seconds for the scalpel to work its way through the various layers of muscle, fat, gristle; enlarging the hole that the weapon had made, so Bones could work the business-end of the anabolic protoplaser in close enough to heal the slashed vena cava. Another sixty seconds to close up. By that time McCoy's two helpers looked worse than the patient— slightly green under splashed red.

"She'll live. But she mustn't be moved, not for about a day."

"I'll stay and guard her," Moore said.

"No," Wilson said. "You're faster than I am; that might make a real difference if there's another fracas. Besides, I'm old enough to be her father. She wouldn't be embarrassed, having me care for her."

"Besides," Moore said, "it's an order."

"I was about to bring that up."

McCoy did a fair job of cleaning the blood off himself, and passed the rag to Wilson. Kirk was talking in a low tone, reporting the situation to Uhura. Larousse stood with the phaser in his hand, trembling some, covering the magician.

"I don't understand," he said. "It was set on 'stun.'"

McCoy was standing over the shattered body of the guard who had attacked Park. "Guess you couldn't see from where you're standing. It was Tinney's phaser that got him, not yours. She must not've checked the setting, or maybe it spun up to a high number when she drew."

"That's . . . something of a relief. I've never killed anybody. Not what I joined for."

"I don't think Tinney's killed anyone, either. Not even now. Isn't that true, magician?" He prodded the remains with his toe. "This one will be back in no time, right?"

"I don't know what you mean by 'no time.' His new body will be quickened soon, but it will be many twenties of days before he can resume his responsibilities. *Ela* learn faster than our lower brothers, but we have so much more to learn, since we keep our memories."

The magician paused. "Is this why you are angry with me? Is it really true, that you are never replaced?"

"Yes, it's true; yes, that's why we're angry! You came within a centimeter of killing that girl—"

"Nonsense word."

"—and she'd never come back." He turned from the grisly scene in front of him and looked at the magician. "Girls. A girl, or woman, or female, is the same species as a boy, or man, or male. The basic constituents of life are different, though. Your standard model girl is made of sugar and spice and everything nice. Boys, on the other hand, are made of sticks and snails and puppy-dog tails. *Kapish?*"

"I don't understand any of that."

"Well, it makes as much sense as this 'replacement' mumbo-jumbo. You clone them, don't you."

"Of course not."

"You know what a clone is, though."

"Certainly. We clone many varieties of plants and animals. It's not the same as replacement, though.

"Look at this, for instance." He pointed to a thick white ridge that ran diagonally across his wing. "This is a scar I got from your brother Klingons, ten generations ago. A clone of me, if we were to clone Chatalia —let alone *ela!*—wouldn't have the scar. No more than it would have my memories, my individuality."

"You're talking about immortality, which we know is impossible." (Some humans had "serial immortality"—replacing organs as they wore out—but after a couple of hundred years you couldn't coax the cells to divide properly, and everything fell apart at once.) "I think you're deluded. Or lying to us."

"Magicians do not lie," he said.

"That may be so," Spock said. "Neither this one nor T'Lallis has said anything that was demonstrably untrue, at least according to their own view of the world."

"Let me try to explain. It is not that we live forever. We are replaced as long as we are useful. Whole families have been allowed to die out when their function has become obsolete; individuals are allowed to die without replacement if their behavior indicates that their future survival would be a liability to the rest."

"That still doesn't explain what you do," McCoy said. "How do you duplicate yourselves, if it's not cloning?"

"The Father Machine." The magician gestured at the torn-up body that floated near McCoy's feet. "That one, for instance, his name is T'Kyma. The next time I go Below, I will tell the Father Machine that T'Kyma is to be replaced.

"We go to the Father Machine every twentieth day, and sit with it for a while. When we die, or are so ill that we must be killed, the Machine produces a copy of what we were, last time we sat with it."

"Memories and all," Bones said.

"For the *ela*, yes. The *ven* and *lan* are replaced by a different Father Machine, which only reproduces the physical body. There are *lan* families that specialize in educating these new ones."

"I would like to see this Father Machine," Spock said.

"There are a lot of machines I'd like to see," Kirk added. "Will you take us to them?"

"Below?"

"Wherever. You were going to take us somewhere with these guards, weren't you?"

"Yes, and Below, as a matter of fact. But not to show you things."

"Suppose we go there now," Kirk said. "Armed."

Scotty had rationed the bottle, one drink every forty-five minutes, and was sober as Spock. He didn't especially want to be sober, but he did want to save enough for one final toast, watching the bomb come in.

In Scott's university days, in Glasgow, he had spent a certain amount of time in pubs. There had been a custom then, and may be a custom still, to determine who would pay for the next round of drinks: the boy who had paid for the previous round would stand (banging a glass on the table, for punctuation) and recite the first line of a poem, Scottish usually;

sometimes English. The one to his left had to supply the second line; the one to *his* left, the third, and so on. The first one to muff a line bought the table.

Scotty thought it a mark of a gentleman to allow others to pay for one's liquor—and a man who can memorize every line of a complicated technical drawing can memorize a few lines of verse.

To keep from drinking alone, Scotty had been for a couple of hours reciting those poems from twenty years ago, summoning up his young comrades. Pacing around the green.

Twelve minutes to go, now. He had to move back to the emergency bridge, warm up the viewscreen. As he stepped into the lift, he began a poem by Robert Graham:

> "If doughty deeds my lady please
> "Right soon I'll mount my steed;
> "And strong his arm, and fast his seat,
> "Tha' bears frae me the meed—"

He let that one go; it seemed inappropriate to celebrate chivalry when your foe was a cruel sniper. Riding the lift, stepping out, he was haunted by dark lines from Donne and Shakespeare, but he wouldn't sing of death, not now. Ten minutes.

He settled into the command chair and turned on the screen. It took him a couple of minutes, at lowest power, to locate the bomb. He watched it come closer, debating with himself, finally not calling Uhura.

With one minute to go, he poured brandy to the rim of the glass, and solemnly drank it off. He scowled at the bomb, growing visibly larger every second.

"Damn you," he whispered to Kulain. He knew

stronger language, but was saying what he meant. "God damn you to Hell."

The screen went impossibly brilliantly white.

The Magicians' Island was a bizarre landscape to walk through. The ground was dry clay that seemed hard as cement, but plants grew everywhere, and in no esthetic or logical pattern. They were all colors of the rainbow—leaves as well as flowers—and came in every size and shape, from small tufts of grass to tortuous coils of thorny vine in clumps the size of houses. As they approached the entrance to Below, the going got rough: thick matted jungle that they had to burn away by phaser. It wasn't designed to be approached on foot, but Kirk and his men had no desire to take to the air. Spock held the magician (whose name, they learned, was T'oomi) firmly by the arm, and pushed him along in front.

The entrance was a carved hole some five hundred meters in diameter. Its sides were black and smooth as if carved from obsidian; there were no steps, of course.

"You lead, T'oomi," Kirk said. "I can't really threaten you, since you believe you can't die." He wiped dirty sweat from his face, panting with the past hour's exertion. "But before you give any thought to escaping, or not cooperating in every way . . . think of what these weapons could do to the Father Machine. And the rest of Below."

"I understand," the magician said. "And I will be cooperative . . . but I don't think—"

"Captain!" Spock said, a queer note in his voice. "Look at the time."

Kirk knew what Spock meant before he saw the numbers. "We're alive."

"The shell must have worked."

"Scotty . . ." Kirk whipped out his communicator. "Kirk to *Enterprise*. Come in, Mr. Scott."

There was nothing but static. He put the communicator away. "Get moving," he said, and took a step toward T'oomi.

"Don't touch!" The magician flapped away. He hovered over the edge of the pit. "Follow me."

"We'll walk," Kirk said. "You stay right in front of us." They started fly-walking down the smooth wall, toward what looked like a dense garden below.

It took nearly a half-hour to get there. It was easier going than the jungle had been, but the illusion of constantly defying gravity was disorienting and tiring.

The half-kilometer-wide hole was essentially an air shaft for Below, which was a huge buried dome tens of kilometers in extent. A cold bluish light emanated uniformly from the featureless ceiling. They drifted down cautiously, phasers drawn, Moore with the heavy phaser rifle.

Below looked like a formal garden gone to seed. There were plants in neat circular and polygonal beds, but weeds and vines sprawled everywhere. The variety of sizes, shapes, and colors was as great as they'd seen above, but in this cool dim light it all seemed sinister.

When they came to the floor, they bounced. The tractor boots wouldn't hold. "T'oomi?" Kirk said. "What is this?" T'oomi just floated there, looking at them. "Spock?"

"Interesting . . . there are a few substances that repel tractor fields, but they are all metallic." The floor looked like a conglomerate of gravel and cement.

"It's more complicated than that," Larousse said. "Check the time."

Spock and Kirk looked at their chronometers, and the faces were blank. Kirk drew out his communicator and flipped it open; there was no bleat to indicate activation.

"Kirk to Uhura." Silence.

T'oomi said something in Chatalian, and the translator was mute.

"My God," McCoy said. "Nothing works down here."

From every direction, magicians were sliding toward them through the air. Most of them were armed.

12

Scotty had rubbed the glare from his eyes and pinched himself hard, and decided that either (1) he was alive, or (2) the afterlife was rather prosaic.

"Uhura to *Enterprise*. Come in, please!" The message was weak and full of static.

"This is the *Enterprise*. I'm all richt, Uhura!"

"*Enterprise*, come in, please." She didn't hear him. "*Please* come in!"

"Kirk to *Enterprise*. Come in, Mr. Scott." The captain's signal was even fainter.

"I'm here, Captain!" He was shouting. "The ship made it through!"

Disgusted, he turned off the communicator. There wasn't enough power to maintain the neutrino carrier wave.

He felt a cold chill that was simultaneously one of scary revelation and actual physical coolness. If there wasn't enough power to run a communicator, how long could the life support systems run?

It felt like the temperature of the emergency bridge had dropped at least ten degrees, since he'd seen the bomb go off. If it kept falling at this rate, he'd freeze solid before long.

He leaped out of the chair and ran to the turbolift. He would have to gather some food and water from the entertainment area. Other things. Blankets—

The lift didn't come. Not enough power.

Scotty forced the doors open. There was a gangway that would normally take him down the one deck necessary, but it was connected to the parts of the ship that were without life support. Fortunately, the elevator shaft was sealed, and there were rungs connecting the decks. He clambered down and forced open the Deck Eight doors. Have to move fast; get everything together and then shut it all down, everything but the Bridge. Pity about the trees.

There must have been two hundred of the aliens, all with the gold ribbon of first caste. T'oomi was talking to them in a loud orator's voice.

"Can you understand any of that, Larousse?" Kirk asked.

"Nothing useful. I understand the word for 'magician' and the word for us, or Klingons, maybe. It's a different language than the one T'Lallis used."

"Do you want me to make a break for it?" Moore suggested. "I can probably outrun them, in a straight line."

"If they just had the spears, might be a good idea," Kirk said. "But some of those in the back have bows."

"That doesn't mean they could hit me."

"Let's not take the chance." One Chatalia was swimming toward them, weaponless, but with an armful of what looked like bunches of celery, dark blue. "Get ready for something."

There were fiber loops threaded through the bases of the blue celery; the magician approached Kirk and slowly passed the loop over his head, the stalks hanging there like a vegetable necktie.

"Now," the alien said, "can you understand me?"

"Uh," Kirk said, nonplussed. "Uh . . . yes, I do. You understand me?"

"Of course." He moved to McCoy.

"What the hell is going on here?" McCoy tried to brush him away.

"Translators," Kirk said, but what McCoy heard was "Grunfoon w'kaiba."

"Oh, I get it." He cooperated, as did the others.

When Larousse got his, he said, "How did you do this?"

"I didn't do it. Don't you remember? The Father Machine made them. Last time you came."

"Wait. These work with Klingon?"

"Of course."

"Copan yopoo opundoperstopand mopee?" *Can you understand me?*

"Sure." He swam away.

"They're *better* than ours," he said to Spock. "They don't have to be calibrated to one language."

"*Je parle français,*" Spock said. "*Pouvez-vous me comprendre?*"

"I hear that in French," Larousse said, "but I understand French. *Wakarimasu ka?*"

"That, I heard in Vulcan. 'Do you understand?' "

"It was Japanese. What an incredible machine."

"Telepathic," Spock said, looking at the stalks

with interest. "Similar to ours, really, except for being plants."

T'oomi was talking. ". . . and when they die, it is always death-without-replacement. This is also suspicious.

"But I have been with them for some time, and a second-caste one who traveled with them for days agrees with me: they don't act at all the way I remember Klingons."

Kirk spoke up. "We are not Klingons. The physical similarities are superficial. Your scientists, your 'life arts' people, could examine us and tell you that right away."

There was a long ringing silence. "The Father Machine," someone in the crowd said.

"That would be possible," T'oomi said. He turned to the crew. "You might not survive it, though. The Father Machine killed every Klingon we sent to it. Without replacement."

"Do you know why it killed them?" Kirk said.

"Because they endangered the order of things."

"Not because they were . . . evil?"

"That word doesn't translate."

"Ah. I suppose we also upset the order of things."

"You certainly have. Whether that would cause the Machine to kill you, I can't know."

"Let me suggest an alternative," Spock said. "You know that my touch, unlike the others', doesn't harm you."

"So far as we know."

"Very well. My people, Vulcans, have a special gift called 'mind touch.' It allows an intimate telepathic connection between two beings, where there can be no falsehood, no slightest misrepresentation. Would one of you agree to enter into this with me?"

"Can others monitor this?" T'oomi asked.

"No. It's a personal communication, one-to-one."

T'oomi sculled toward him. "There is danger involved, though."

"It is painful to both. Not necessarily dangerous."

"I will try."

Spock's long, graceful fingers touched the alien's temples. Kirk grimaced, watching. He had seen this done before, and knew what a toll it exacted from his friend.

But as the minutes passed, Spock just floated there, a frown of intense concentration on his face. No sign of pain.

He let go of T'oomi, puzzled. "Nothing. Somehow, you must be capable of blocking the process."

"I haven't resisted. But I also felt nothing." He floated away, turning his back. "I think the Vulcan, as he calls himself, was lying. Like a *ven* or *lan,* or Klingon."

Kulain sat tensely in the command chair, and viewed the crystal again, perhaps for the twentieth time. It showed the nova bomb falling in toward the planetoid, dropping so it would detonate right beside the *Enterprise*.

"Slow it down, now," he said to the communications officer. "Slow it down as much as you can."

The image of the *Enterprise* took up nearly half the screen. The bomb came to within two or three hundred meters, and suddenly became a white dot, painfully bright, that began to grow. The fireball

swelled until it touched the surface of the planetoid
—and then it suddenly disappeared.

"Impossible!" Kulain raged. "Energy can't disappear like that."

The Klingon beside him, the ordnance officer,
nodded uneasily. "The fireball should have grown to
envelope the planetoid . . . and then grown ten times
more. And take many hours to dissipate."

"So what happened?"

He frowned at the screen. "Magic."

"Lieutenant . . ."

"I'm serious, sire. It might as well be. The laws of
heat dynamics are at the very root of all our science.
This denies them. So 'magic' is adequate, as a functional description."

"I want a counterweapon, not a 'functional description.' "

"Of course, sire." He thought for a moment. "The
first thing we have to decide is whether this defensive
weapon was deployed by the *Enterprise* or by these
Chatalia."

"If the *Enterprise,* their distress signal was a hoax
to lure us in, goad us into attacking," Kulain mused.
"Perhaps to test their device. And put us in a situation
that might prove embarrassing in terms of the Organian
treaty."

"If the signal was real, though," the ordnance officer said, "it does contain testimony that the Chatalia
have some mysterious mastery over energy. Magic."

"Offensive word." He leaned back and closed his
eyes. "What we need is a plan of action that would be
appropriate in either case. Ideas?"

After a long silence, the officer said, "Perhaps I
lack imagination. All I can think of is a direct assault,

via transporter. Force the secret out of them, perhaps, before wiping them out."

Kulain hadn't changed expression. Now he smiled thinly and opened his eyes. "You are fortunate that your post does not *require* imagination. We have one nova bomb left, correct?"

"Yes, sire. But I wouldn't advise—"

"No, we won't repeat the same action. We use the transporter. Detonate the bomb *inside* the planetoid."

"But, sire . . . the bomb is too large to be transported."

Kulain tapped the side of his head. "Imagination, Lieutenant. We send it in piecemeal. We also transport a team of experts, to reassemble and detonate it."

"An ordnance team, sire?"

"Would you trust the cooks with it?"

"Right away, sire." The ordnance officer stood, rather slowly, and saluted. "Survive and succeed."

Kulain watched him go, then turned to study the crystal once more. Of course, he thought, there was another course of action consistent with either explanation: flee. Distressingly human thought. Maybe Kal was right. Obscene. But there's dark pleasure in thinking it.

The magicians had taken away their celery-stalk translators so they couldn't overhear, and were engaged in lively debate, presumably over what to do with them. T'oomi had remarked that this group comprised every single first-caste magician, which was a gathering that occurred only a few times per generation.

"If there's anything like a control room down here," Kirk said, "it's pretty well camouflaged."

"It's possible we are looking for the wrong thing,"

Spock said. "I have a theory: all of their machines may be in the form of plants—remember, T'Lallis said that 'tending plants' was the main activity of the first-castes."

"Plant machines, though?"

"It makes sense. Suppose you were planning a vessel like this, one that would be in flight for tens of thousands of years, maybe more. What would be your main concern?"

Kirk rubbed his chin. "I think I see. Maintenance. No place to get spare parts, and almost nothing will go that long without breaking down."

"Exactly. But if you are advanced enough in life sciences to create plants that duplicate the functions of your machines, then you can make exact replacements by simple methods of plant propagation."

Larousse joined them. "If that's so, it's possible that none of them *does* know they're on a spaceship. If they had a strong tradition that every plant is to be cared for and eventually replaced, thus-and-so . . ."

The chatter was quieting down. "It should be easy enough to find out," Kirk said. "Here comes T'oomi." It was difficult to tell one from another, normally, but T'oomi had the identifying scar on his wing. Another *ela* accompanied him, with their translators.

"T'oomi, tell us," Kirk said, "are the plants really—"

"We will talk later, maybe. First you go to the Father Machine. Follow me."

It was a nervous-making trip. Each of the crew members had a spear-carrying escort directly behind him, and a phalanx of bowmen followed. They flew very slowly.

As Spock would have predicted, the Father Ma-

chine was a plant, or a system of plants. It rose fifty
meters off the ground, and was as big around as it was
high. Blue-green leaves larger than a man, thorn-
pointed, overlapped one another as do those of an artichoke, but with striking regularity. It looked like a cross
between an artichoke and a spiral staircase, the size of
an office building. As they approached, they could see
motion: it seemed to be breathing.

They stopped near the top of it, and found that
indeed it was breathing, in warm regular gusts. Its
breath smelled disturbingly of rotten meat.

"What does this thing eat?" Kirk asked.

"Anything it wants," said T'oomi.

In the assembly area adjacent to the transporter
room, Kulain was inspecting his troops. There were
two groups: the ordnance team, with a heavy-weap-
ons squad for protection, and a group of priests and
scientists (heavily armed, for tradition's sake), who
were to beam down to the ruin of the ancient Klingon
vessel.

Kulain himself planned to beam aboard the *Enterprise*. Their sensors said that one man had stayed
behind. Kulain wanted to meet him, to indulge his interest in human psychology; perhaps to kill him, in an
appropriate way. Some way that would not be "aggression" in Organian terms.

"This will be the order of transport. First, the
ordnance team, with their guard. The parts of the nova
bomb will follow directly.

"You will go to the leading pole. There is no centrifugal gravity there, so it will be easy to handle the
machinery."

He addressed the highest-ranking priest in the next

group. "Then you go, and you'll be quick about it. If we can believe the distress message from the Federation ship, we may be close enough to be snared by whatever trapped them." Kulain would leave right after.

Scotty sat with his back against the dais of the useless transporter, wrapped in four layers of blanket. In front of him, a small fire burned brightly, the only source of light in the emergency bridge room.

To his left was a stack of wood: uprooted saplings, branches hacked off larger trees (which he'd done with a tritanium axe from a cabinet of emergency fire supplies—it could slice through metal doors, and made short work of wood), and some chunks of exotic furniture. To his right, seventeen bottles of compressed oxygen. The eighteenth, he had propped between his knees, regulator barely cracked, nozzle pointing toward the fire. A forgotten bottle of brandy sat beside him, frozen to slush. It was forty degrees below zero. In the rest of the ship it was much colder.

Flickering at first, then solid, Kulain appeared. Scotty had his eyes closed, trying to rest.

"Human!" Kulain said, then coughed spasmodically. Klingons had slightly better tolerance to low temperatures than humans, but not this low. "Are you alive?" he croaked.

"Aye, the last time I took a readin' . . . though I ken *you* won't be lastin' long, in this bitterness."

Kulain inhaled sharply; frost in his throat cut off his reply. He unsnapped the flap of his holster.

"Don' do that." Scotty's outstretched arm bulged the blanket in front of him. "I'll blast ye away."

Kulain said something in Klingon, loudly. He flickered slightly, but didn't go away.

"If ye're tryin' to transport, give it up. Ye're stuck here."

"Stuck?"

Scotty nodded. "Mebbe for good."

The Klingon looked at him blankly for a moment, then seemed to slump. "Don't you shoot." He slowly drew his weapon and put it against his forehead. When he pulled the trigger, it made a sound like a tired kitten.

"This doesn't work, either?"

"Nope. Nor would this phaser, if it were real." The blanket dropped away, revealing a bare hand. "Ye're welcome to share these blankets with me, if ye'll take a turn at tendin' the fire."

"I'd rather die." He folded his arms across his chest.

"Suit yerself." Scotty drew the blankets around himself. "Fat lot of good you do your fatherland, frozen stiff. Hold yer breath until ye turn blue, I don' care."

A minute later, he said, "All right," through chattering teeth. He picked up a sapling and broke it in two (with a brittle sound like ceramic breaking), laid a piece on the fire, and set the other half nearby. The blankets encircled both of them, so long as they stayed shoulder-to-shoulder.

Kulain stared morosely into the fire. "I've never been so close to a human that I could smell him."

"You ain't no bloody bunch of posies, yerself."

13

"I will go first," Spock said.

"Wait—" Kirk was cut off by T'oomi.

"No. It must be a human. There are twenty twenties of you gathered in the gardens of *lan*. We have to know what to do with you."

"I'll do it," Moore said. "I'm the most dispensable."

"Moore," Kirk said, struggling between logic and emotion, "I would never order you to . . ."

"I know, sir. Maybe that's why I can volunteer." He floated up toward T'oomi. "Besides. It looks like we're all dead, anyhow."

"Oracles," said T'oomi. Two magicians presented themselves. "Ready him—as well as you can, without touching his skin."

They told Moore to be still, and keep his arms at his sides. Then, only touching his chest, they pushed him toward the purple blossom at the top of the Father Machine.

One of the oracles whistled a series of notes, and the blossom opened. They guided Moore into it, and the petals closed around him.

After about ten seconds, the blossom expelled him violently, sneezing him toward the ceiling. Two guards took after him; he met them halfway, flying back down.

One of the oracles fit himself halfway into the blossom, head and shoulders sticking out. In a singsong voice he said:

"Not Klingon. Klingons taste good, have unpleasant minds. This one tastes poison, but his mind is neutral. Where is the one that claims to be a different species?"

Spock drifted over. "Can you warn it I'm half-human?"

"It knows," T'oomi said. "It knows everything about you that T'Lallis did."

"Will the communication be both ways?"

"No, the Father Machine only speaks through the oracle family." It had never encountered a Vulcan before, though. Spock decided he would try mind touch with it.

The inside of the blossom was white and shiny with moisture, like the mouth of a snake. Spock let them ease him inside. As it closed over him, he put out his palms and did the mental twist that would initiate mind touch.

He screamed.

"Don't fire unless they show some sign of aggression," Uhura said. About a hundred *lan* were approaching them, a silent mob. A dozen or so had spears, but many of the others carried farming tools that would make effective weapons.

Leading them was an unarmed ven-Chatalia, with the three blue ribbons of a no-caste interpreter. Uhura turned on the translator. "Uh, hello," she said uncertainly.

The mob stopped dead. A hundred whispering voices sounded like a cloud of insects chirring. The interpreter huddled with a couple of the spear-bearers, who talked to higher-caste spear-bearers, and relayed some message back to the interpreter. The little *ven* came forward, obviously intimidated by the tall black woman.

"We won't hurt you," Uhura said. "We welcome a chance to talk with you."

"I bear a message," he said.

"From?"

"From the farmers of this village, and their protectors. You are destroying their land. You must leave."

"We have been careful not to disturb the crops, other than the ones we harvested to make room."

"But your touching them made them poisonous on the outside. And the poisons from your bodies are spreading through the soil." True, the plants nearest the latrine had started turning green—probably not a sign of health, in a blue cabbage.

"But if we move, we'll only poison some other area."

"Then it would not be my problem any more," he said logically. Suddenly, he looked up.

Three magicians coasted down from the sky. One of them landed between Uhura and the interpreter. Ignoring the woman, he towered over the *ven*. "What in the name of Below are you doing?"

"These *lan*, mine, they have, the soil . . ."

"Didn't you come from the city?"

"Yes, master."

"Don't you know you are to take no notice of these magicians from the future? That they can harm you?"

"Yes, master."

"Do you know you have marked yourself for death without replacement?"

"Please, master." He dropped his voice. "You know how it is with these—"

The magician picked him up by the loose skin behind his shoulders and hurled him toward the spearbearers. "Kill him," he said, and turned to Uhura. "As for you—"

The magician, the interpreter, the "protectors," and about thirty of the *lan,* all fell over stunned. The rest of the *lan* stampeded back toward the village. The other two magicians took to the air; one of them pulled a long silver knife from his pouch.

He dove toward Uhura, but it was an unequal contest. Uhura calmly stunned him in midair—and he fell hard, landing on his head with a loud snap.

"Drop the other one?" a Security man asked, tracking the magician as he rose.

"No," Uhura said. "I think we've done enough damage, for today."

Nurse Chapel was leaning over the still form of the fallen magician. Uhura rushed over. "Dead?"

She nodded. "This is passing strange." Holding its top-hair by thumb and forefinger, she gently moved the head back and forth. It went in any direction, without offering resistance. "Would it be all right if I did an autopsy?"

Uhura hesitated. "I suppose . . . first let's put up some sheets or something. So the village doesn't see."

Uhura had no great desire to watch; she was playing a slow game of Owari with Sulu when Chapel finished. She walked up as if in a daze, still holding her bloody gloves.

"Incredible." She sat down. "I wish Spock were here."

Uhura rattled a handful of pebbles; looked at the nurse with curiosity and concern. "What did you find?"

"It's got no central nervous system at all. Just a suffusion of minor ganglia. No spinal cord, no brain."

The Father Machine ate Spock, dissolving him the way a transporter dissolves people, but not as quickly; and then recreated him, as a transporter also does.

Watching the destruction of himself was rather horrifying, Spock thought, but the opposite process was fascinating.

—You are trying to talk to me.

Yes. To tell you the truth, so you can pass it on to the magicians.

—I know all truth. The magicians have no need of it.

You know you are inside a spaceship?

—Laughing. I built it. I am the pilot.

Do you know that you are doomed?

—Still laughing. Really?

If your present course is not changed, you will come to rest in a volume of space light-years away from any star.

—I lived near a star once. It exploded.

But understand: if you don't have a star nearby, you will run out of energy. Eventually you will cool down, to nearly absolute zero.

—Laughing. *You* need a star nearby, you mean. *Then what will you do for energy?*

—You may have noticed. Your starship is low on energy. I drained it. I am in the process of draining another now.

But you can't count on starships showing up regularly, forever.

—I have other resources. Although it's boring, and takes all of my attention, I can convert matter directly to energy. There is enough dust between the stars to keep me alive indefinitely. In lean times, I can consume my own substance, and recreate it when there is excess energy.

As you consume the Chatalia?

—Occasionally, yes. As you suspect, they are not truly alive. They are toys for me; it pleases me to watch them.

Does it please you to watch us?

—In small doses, yes. You are putting too much disorder in the system now. I will have to be rid of you.

You would kill us all?

—I haven't decided. You seem fairly sentient. At any rate, I wouldn't have to kill you; if I ignore you, you will die soon enough.

Same thing. It was you who trapped us here.

—You who trapped yourselves. You weren't invited.

With that, Spock was suddenly in the open air, tumbling, two magicians chasing after him. They flew back to the blossom, where an oracle was fitting himself into the space Spock had vacated.

"How was it, Spock?" Kirk asked.

Spock answered sotto voce: "The Father Machine

claims to be the only sentient creature on this vessel—"

"But our biosensor data—"

"Were ambiguous. I have a theory . . ."

The oracle began talking. "I think I may let you people go back to where you came from. Two conditions: first, that you never come back here.

"Second, I am hungry for Klingons. There are a few here now. Send me the rest. You know what I mean."

"That would be murder," Kirk said.

"No, Captain," Spock said. "Allow me to take care of it."

"In fact, those few Klingons approach Below now. There has been some fighting. They brought a gift of energy."

The nova bomb they'd assembled was a blocky piece of gray metal, about the size of a shuttlecraft. They had pushed it through the air shaft with back-pack rockets; it would hit the floor of Below in less than a minute.

"Is that what I think it is?" Kirk said.

"Perhaps less," Spock said. "We should be in no danger. Unless there is a limit to the amount of energy it can absorb."

"Not much we can do about it, at any rate."

They both stared at the bomb's slow progress. Nine Klingons accompanied it, dressed in funereal space suits. As they passed out of the air shaft, their rockets fizzled out, and they showed signs of distress— their life support systems failing—until they could get their helmets off.

"Bring them to me," the oracle said. "Escort these others away."

The Klingons floated with stiff dignity, expecting to be vaporized any second. When the nova bomb crunched harmlessly into the gravel, they had a swift conference, then eight of them formed a Klingon Square, blasters out, while the ninth opened a plate on the side of the bomb and tinkered with it. All of them swam clumsily, without wings.

As the *Enterprise* crew passed over them, the Klingons found out that their blasters didn't function. They also tried them on the phalanx of spearmen that approached. Then they drew knives and formed in a line.

When the crew from the *Enterprise* glided into the air shaft, their guard peeled away, presumably to strike the Klingons from behind. Their tractor boots worked again; it was a relief to walk.

Communicator bleeped. "Kirk here."

"This is Mr. Scott, sir. We seem to have power. Would you like me to beam you up?"

"Check Lieutenant Uhura, see whether she has any sick or wounded. Otherwise . . ." He looked back at the Klingons, getting ready for futile combat; looked ahead at the weird sun that would float forever inside this eternally stagnant world. "Beam me up *yesterday!*"

14

Captain Kirk tried to keep a straight face as he stepped down from the transporter in the emergency bridge. It didn't resemble any bridge he had ever commanded: a smoldering campfire, a couple of uprooted trees, food containers scattered everywhere. A couple of empty brandy bottles. A Klingon.

"Captain Quirk, I prezhume?" A drunk Klingon. "I am Captain Kulain, of the war, warship *Korezima*." He folded his arms on his chest and swayed slightly.

He flickered. "Oops! Time to go. Goodbye, Mr. Scott." His brow furrowed. "Can't . . . think of the word. Ah. Thank you."

"My pleasure." The Klingon disappeared.

"Looks like you've been entertaining, Scotty."

Scott finished adjusting dials and turned to Kirk. "It's a long story, sir."

"A good one, too, I'll bet."

"They're not such bad folks, once you get to know them. Can't hold their liquor, though."

"How did you get him to take a drink? I thought they didn't do *anything* for pleasure."

"No' for pleasure, sir. For temperature regulation.

It was so cold we had to thaw out the brandy." He checked a readout. "Be at least five minutes before the transporter room's warmed up, sir. Would you like me to beam up Mr. Spock?"

"Sure. I want to see his face."

No satisfaction there. He stepped down poker-faced. "It must have been very cold, Mr. Scott. I'm glad you are all right."

He went to the viewscreen. "Can you put me in contact with the Klingon vessel?"

"Aye." He fiddled with some switches.

"Spock—are you actually going to deliver—"

"I gave my word, Captain. But actually . . ."

A dim figure appeared. "This is Kal, temporarily in command. Who calls?"

"This is the star ship *Enterprise,* Science Officer Spock here. I have a warning for you.

"The dominant creature in the planetoid below, which calls itself the Father Machine, has issued a challenge: it wishes to consume every one of you.

"I strongly urge that you not answer the challenge. None of your weapons will work in his domain and he may be able to prevent you from ever returning to your ship."

"Knives will work, though, and bare hands, no?"

"True, but you will be greatly outnumbered."

It was hard to read expressions through the swirling colors, but it looked like Kal had a smug smile. "Good." He switched off.

"You see, Captain. Nothing but the truth."

The Father Machine had returned enough fuel for them to reach Starbase 3. Kirk put the crew on light-duty status and everyone settled in to loaf for a week.

Several of the officers were sharing a bottle of Saurian brandy in the lounge. "I wish we could go back, in safety," Spock said. "So many questions unanswered."

"This rebirth thing?" Bones said.

"No, not especially. That's really just regeneration, with the help of something like transporter technology. Since the Chatalia are actually only extensions of the Father Machine. Like limbs."

"Seems pretty impressive to me," Kirk said.

"Other creatures do it," Spock said, "usually on a smaller scale. The real mystery has to do with *energy*. What the Father Machine does defies the basic laws of thermodynamics, and conservation of energy. Since he does *do* it, our laws are wrong. Insufficient."

Wilson came in and pulled up a chair. "Just came from seeing Ensign Tinney, in sick bay. Chapel says she'll be up in a couple of days."

"Don't suppose you've seen Ensign Moore," Bones said.

"As a matter of fact, he was there, too. He was reading to her." Bones rolled his eyes ceilingward but didn't say anything.

"I guess we owe you a real debt, Mr. Spock," Wilson said. "They tell me if you hadn't been able to talk to that overgrown artichoke, we'd all still be down there. Dead, probably."

"It was the logical thing to try," Spock said. "And really not unpleasant, compared to other experiences with mind touch. As I was just telling these people, I wish I could spend more time with him. It."

"You had a lot in common with it," Bones said, expressionlessly.

"It was not the similarities that made it attractive. It seemed to be logical, for instance, but valid logic is invariant from species to species."

Spock stared into space. "No, what was most interesting about it was its humor. I believe it was the only truly intelligent creature I've ever met that had a sense of humor."

After a moment of silence, McCoy said, "There you go again."

"What do you mean?"

"If anybody else had said that, I would swear it was a joke."

Spock arched an eyebrow at him. "One of us is learning something."

Author's Note

Since this is probably my last Star Trek book, I ought to take a page and thank the people who helped me with both of them: the Science Fiction League of Iowa Students, especially Sue Weinberg, who helped keep my stories consistent with the TV series (I was overseas when most of it was aired); Miss Sheila Clark, who supplied authentic dialect for Scotty; Dr. Gregory Benford, who helped me figure out what happens to bodies of water inside a planetoid such as the one in *World Without End;* Gay and Sydny, for quiet patience; Gene Roddenberry, who not only let me take liberties with his creations, but even suggested a few.

A SMALL CONTEST:

The day *Planet of Judgment* (Bantam Books, New York, 1977) came out, I realized with horror that there was a grievous mistake on the very first page. I waited for a deluge of letters.

Well, there were plenty of letters, but none about that. So it's not too obvious a mistake.

Here's a hint: it has to do with a word that

sounds similar to my name. If you see the error, write me care of this publisher. First two correct respondents win autographed copies of my first novel, long out-of-print in hardback, and presumably valuable.

This offer expires 31 December 1978, is void where prohibited by law, and is a cheap trick to make you read *Planet of Judgment*.

Finally, a matter that might be of interest to science fiction readers. To assure that the wording of the quotation beginning this book was correct, I picked up the telephone and called Arthur C. Clarke—who lives on an island in the Indian Ocean, literally halfway around the world. I heard him quite clearly, though my own voice generated a faint feedback echo, characteristic of communication via satellite.

Clarke was the first one to suggest the possibility of using satellites for global communication, in a *Wireless World* article in 1945. I wonder if he could have predicted that it would be commonplace, so soon.

And it makes you wonder what magics will be commonplace tomorrow.

—JOE HALDEMAN

Florida, 1978

ABOUT THE AUTHOR

Joe Haldeman has written almost twenty books and a few dozen short stories, novelettes, and novellas since 1970 when he started writing full-time. He has won both the Hugo and Nebula Awards for best novel for *The Forever War* (1975) and for best novella "The Hemingway Hoax" (1990). He also won the Hugo for Best Science Fiction Short Story for "Tricentennial" (1976). He writes songs and poetry, nonfiction articles and editorials, but will only write criticism in which he can praise writers without reservation. He adapted *The Forever War* for the stage and it opened in 1983 in Chicago performed by the Organic Theater Company. A short story, "I of Newton" appeared on the *Twilight Zone* television show in 1985. He is presently working on two new novels and a short story collection. In his spare time, he enjoys traveling, omnivorous and indiscriminate reading, cooking for daily relaxation, casino gambling, amateur astronomy, a lot of bicycling and a little fishing, canoeing, swimming, snorkeling, drawing and painting, gardening, and guitar playing. He lives in Florida with his wife, Gay.